VAMPIRE BROTHER

STEVE STEPHENSON

Black Rose Writing | Texas

First printing

This is a work of fiction. Names, characters, businesses, places, events, and
incidents are either the products of the author's imagination or used in a
fictitious manner. Any resemblance to actual persons, living or dead, or
actual events is purely coincidental.

ISBN: 978-1-68433-733-0
PUBLISHED BY BLACK ROSE WRITING
www.blackrosewriting.com

Printed in the United States of America
Suggested Retail Price (SRP) $17.95

Vampire Brother is printed in Garamond

*As a planet-friendly publisher, Black Rose Writing does its best to eliminate
unnecessary waste to reduce paper usage and energy costs, while never
compromising the reading experience. As a result, the final word count vs. page count
may not meet common expectations.

Editor- Rob Carr, Cover Art-Caleb Designs

VAMPIRE
BROTHER

CHAPTER ONE

Tarquin and Ress were deep in the forest of Ravannhiel, the stronghold of the wood elves. The two humans had ridden from Menelwyn, the capital, in hopes of getting a little privacy and of enjoying what the forest had to offer. They had camped near a crystal-clear waterfall and were reclining on the grassy bank, listening to the noises of the forest, when suddenly the chirping of the birds died down. The forest went completely silent and even the sounds of the waterfall seemed to dim.

Tarquin reached for his sword, Dragon Bolt, but his bare feet slipped on the deep wet moss. His half fall saved his life when the blade that now slashed well above his head would otherwise have beheaded him. He rose and quickly cut the legs out from under his attacker.

Ress had jumped to her feet and her short sword cut left and then right in a furious duel with a gigantic, white-skinned orc.

Even though he had never actually seen one, Tarquin recognized from the legends he had heard that these orcs were from the West. He engaged another carrying a halberd, its muscles bulging. The huge orc swung his weapon as if the halberd weighed nothing.

Ress dispensed with her first adversary and scrambled up to the flat ground where two more orcs of prodigious size awaited her. She ducked one thrust and jabbed her sword into the orc's stomach. It wheeled away, clutching its mid-section, and the second one stuck Ress in the thigh with its blade, knocking her back down the small hill to the water's edge.

Seeing his beloved struck down, Tarquin stepped inside the swing of his adversary's halberd and took the full brunt of the stout wooden pole in his ribs, breaking several. The orc that had struck down Ress was sliding down the hillock after his fallen prey and, biting back his pain, Tarquin slit his adversary's throat and it wheeled backward.

Tarquin then launched himself through the air and knocked the large orc that was after Ress onto its side. The prince stood, shakily, his ribs on fire, holding Dragon Bolt against the orc's throat.

"Who sent you to the forest of Ravannhiel?" he demanded.

The orc laughed.

"Wouldn't you like to know." He kept his mouth clamped shut until Tarquin pressed his sword a little deeper into its neck. The blade began to heat up.

"T'was, the black witch," it finally admitted.

Tarquin saw that this one would not talk anymore and he ran his sword through the orc's heart. He turned toward his beloved. She was trying to get up, but Tarquin could see blood flowing from her thigh.

Tarquin rushed to her, slipping and sliding down the hill, his feet unable to grip the wet ground. He cradled her head on his leg and frantically sought a healing potion from his pocket and he poured it down her throat.

The blood slowed, but it was such a deep cut that the healing draught could only do so much. Tarquin set about tightly wrapping a tourniquet about her thigh.

Two mounted orcs now thundered down the bank of the river, spears lowered, black cloth tied and fluttering behind each spear point. Tarquin jumped to his feet and deflected both the weapons with Dragon Bolt. The orc's horses slid on the mossy bank and came to rest in the shallows of the river. One made a mighty heave and launched his spear at Tarquin, but the prince dodged it and threw his long dagger at the beast.

The dagger struck the orc in the throat, and the creature flipped over its horse into the water with a loud bloody splash. The other charged, the shallow water flying in all directions as its horse battled forward.

When the orc had to slow down to get his mount to climb the river bank, Tarquin struck. He swung the flat of his sword at the horse's head, and the animal reared. The orc thrust his spear at the former borderer, from a special unit of the dwarvan army, in an effort to skewer him. The prince of Parthia easily cut through the ash wood of the spear and as the horse drew closer to the bank, Tarquin jumped knee deep into the water and neatly dispatched its orc rider.

He checked on Ress and seeing that she now fared better, he went to collect their horses and help his soon to be wife up into the saddle sitting before him.

The two humans rode off toward the elven capital at a gallop.

• • • • •

Martish, the daughter of a lesser clan of Illanni, had chosen the military life as a profession. Her father had wanted her to study the dark arts of the Illanni warlocks and sorceresses so as to increase their clan's standing in the eyes of the other dark elves, but in the end her decision disturbed the family little since her father had bred a household full of little dark elves. One of these would elevate his demanding wishes.

Her father's procreation went against their clan's usual slow birth rate, and one night Martish crept out of the household to escape both the myriad of children and her father's disdain for army life.

She flourished as a soldier and quickly rose up the ranks in the Illanni army, battling successfully against countless creatures throughout the underworld. Her quick rise brought attention from her superiors and she was chosen for special assignments to venture above ground on certain nefarious tasks.

Martish quickly learned the ways of the above ground folk, and she and her two hundred soldiers knew how to dress by wearing overlarge cloaks and leather armor that almost completely covered their bodies and kept the yellow sun from blistering their pale skin. She was still pale, but compared to most Illanni, she looked tan.

She had been tasked her current mission to ambush a patrol of high elves, but in her mind the task seemed to have no importance other than to send a dire message to the elves of light. She knew it was not her place to question orders.

Her troops had been riding hard in the knee-deep snow to keep ahead of the hated high elves and their horses' hooves threw dirt and snow up behind them. Luckily, there were no vampires commanding her soldiers, a fate she would have despised, as she had a total lack of respect for the vampires. At times she hated them and what they stood for. If a vampire had accompanied her soldiers, they would have had to guard it while it slept, hidden from the bright rays of the sun, and she would have easily lost track of the high elves.

Martish hated the vampires and their control over the capital city Illan, but she dared not voice her opinion in public for that would have ended in public torture and eventual death.

•   •   •   •   •

As Martish and her command rode onwards she pondered the fate of her race. After the loss of their homeland from the continental shift that had occurred after the destruction of Zeiglon and the three-way split of the elven nations, the Illanni or dark elves had chosen to live beneath the ground in caves and then eventually in the underworld. They had nearly all died of attrition fighting the denizens of the underworld until Taza had come to their rescue.

Betrayal had become the rule with the Illanni. They believed that they had been treated badly and left to rot in the underworld, forgotten by the elves of light. They had survived without any help from their cousins, the Wood Elves and High Elves. Taza might now be vanquished, but Tibersu their new leader had vowed to lead his people to their birthright, which he claimed was to dominate the underworld and spread the cloak of vampirism throughout the nations of the world of Muiria.

Taza had originally given them the strength they needed for domination, but it was the only attribute their false god had bequeathed to the Illanni. Now the Fire of Taza was gone, and they had discovered it had been a farce, simply a rite that turned out to be more showmanship than anything worthwhile. The dark elf vampires now knew they themselves could turn anyone they wanted without engaging in the elaborate ceremony Taza had forced them to perform.

With that knowledge the Illanni vampires began to take what they wanted and who they wanted. Most of the ruling families had already welcomed vampirism and more were being turned as the days passed. Soon Tibersu's dream of a vampiric nation would become reality.

•   •   •   •   •

A large snowflake struck Martish in the eye pulling her from her musings. The map she used for her mission had been taken from a farm she had raided years before. She was not in command then and had secretly taken the map for future use. Otherwise, it would have burned with the rest of the house while the former owners swung from ropes in a nearby tree.

Tibersu, the leader of the dark elves of Illan, wanted to attack the elves in their own county, but that would have caused the high elves to bulk up their security and make them think twice before venturing forth from the forest of Korvanna. Martish did not see the wisdom nor the larger picture of this, but it had been a command straight from Lord Tibersu and she had no desire to upset the vampire lord of Illan.

Pulling the map out of its case, Martish saw a perfect ambush site, a narrow pass no longer than a thousand paces from one end to another. She spurred her company onward, riding hard through the snow and through an even smaller pass, so they could set the trap for the high elves.

Once through the first pass, she angled her soldiers to the northeast by following the directions on the map. Riding out of the misting snow, she spied a roadway across a snow-covered barren landscape, and she drove her soldiers even faster as they moved closer to their prey.

The pass came into sight. She ordered her company to dismount and ready their weapons. She sent two scouts ahead to check the pass itself and they returned and reported that there was no sign of the high elves. All elves had the ability to tread lightly across certain terrain, barely leaving a print, and these scouts had traveled to the other end of the passage without leaving so much as a hint of their passage.

Martish whirled her horse around and faced her troops.

"Secure the horses in those woods over there and cover their tracks. Then go find well-covered positions among the boulders. You'll want a perfect view to the valley floor and the road. I will blow the signal horn once. Then I'll fire on the head of their column. We'll give them five volleys before attacking down the slope. Remember, you are to hold your arrows until that time comes. Disobey me and you will be murdered by my own hand."

Martish was a harsh commander, but her company knew she protected them and kept them from being turned into vampires with their dangerous whims. When they ventured above ground, they did not need a vampire to slow them down, and this was a fact she had argued time and again with her superiors.

The dark elves had just settled among the boulders when the high elves' horsemen entered the valley and stopped on a slab of bare granite that was clear of snow. Riding a white horse and covered head to toe in plate mail, their commander gave a slight gesture as he ordered his own scouts to ride ahead.

Martish waited at the opposite end of the pass, ready to fire her arrows into the mounted elves if they detected anything awry. The scouts appeared and she tightened the string of her bow. They silently scanned the area beyond, but rode rapidly back, throwing clods of snow and dirt into the air and muddying the pristine environment.

It seemed like an eternity before the scouts returned with the column of horsemen close behind.

Martish drew back her bow, the arrow held lightly between her gloved fingers. As one of the scouts craned his neck, looking for danger, she let the arrow fly with a precision only elves possessed. The projectile flew from her bow and knocked the lead elf off his horse. The shaft of Martish's arrow protruded from his right eye socket. The other high elves were taken off guard when their scout pitched off his horse and landed into the snow, and then they heard Martish blow her horn to signal her force to let their arrows fly into the confused elves below them.

Two hundred arrows blackened the sky of the pass as the high elves quickly reacted and their bows sent arrow after arrow at the cliffs of the passage. Their quick response caused many of Martish's troops to topple over dead. The high elves then quickly dismounted and formed a shield wall that faced outward in both directions toward the attackers. The arrows of Martish's warrior's bounced harmlessly off the shields, but sometimes found flesh and knocked the elves backward into the now blood-stained snow.

The Illanni commander fired five arrows and her troops attacked down the sides of the pass. As she bounded down the rocky slope, she saw a great rolling fireball heading toward her troops from a spell created by the trapped high elves. The fireball incinerated every soldier that stood in its way, but Martish had little time to think about that or her soldiers as she bounded from a boulder to land in between two elves.

She drew her sword and gave a quick thrust into the elf in front of her and a backhand slash sent the other down into the bloody snow.

Now she was in the thick of it.

Soon armed combat waged up and down the pass and the echoes of the battle rang clearly in the thin winter air.

Many Illanni fell before they reached the floor of the pass, but enough succeeded. Her troops launched themselves into the high elves, breaking the shield wall in many places. Martish herself vaulted a dead horse to attack a high elf who was turned away from her. She quickly thrust her sword into the high elf's back, neatly skewing her opponent.

There was no quarter being given or received this day between the two hated enemies and Martish entered the fray swinging left and right. Soon she was covered in blood as she fought toward the middle of the engagement.

She passed over the bodies of both Illanni and high elves. She had to stop several times to engage the enemy, but these were quick little encounters that barely registered in her mind after her extensive training took over and her sword danced through the high elves' defense.

Martish reached the area where the commander of the high elves had gathered what was left of his troops to make a last stand, and as she arrived there, a lightning bolt blew a hole in the front of the wall of shields that the high elves held.

Thank the gods she had a warlock with her command, she thought.

The portion of the shield wall she faced in front of her had yet to be broken, though, and the Illanni commander attacked furiously, stabbing over the shields. Finally, she struck downward in frustration and pinned the high elf's foot to the ground. As the elf lost the concentration he needed to hold the shield wall together, Martish gathered her strength and launched herself at the mythril shield held by the wounded high elf.

Around her, elf still grappled with elf on the blood-soaked ground, each trying to gain a superior position. Every elf had given into their base instincts and had fought like uncontrolled elves. All signs of dignity had been set aside.

Gasping for breath, Martish reached the high elf commander, gleaming in his plate mail, and stood before him. She looked around her and saw that her soldiers were finishing off their opponents.

"I thought your kind huddled under the mountains," the high elf sneered.

"Not now. Go to your king and tell him that Tibersu, vampire lord of Illan, goes where he wants. He doesn't forget old indiscretions. Now and forever, you will remain our enemy and will feel our wrath. Surface dweller, go back to your king and deliver that message."

One of the commander's remaining high elves brought a horse to him and as he mounted, Martish swung and decapitated the elf that had brought the horse.

"That is what I think of your kind," she said.

The high elven commander pulled hard on the reins of his horse and galloped away.

Martish turned to look again upon her soldiers. Those that remained upright now swayed in exhaustion.

She sounded the horn and her soldiers headed to the forest, where their horses were tied. Some stopped to help wounded comrades, while others dispatched the wounded enemies lying in the snow.

Martish had entered the battle with two hundred Illanni. She left with little more than a hundred. The high elves had fought well, but she hoped her message was understood.

Otherwise, her soldiers would have died in vain.

CHAPTER TWO

Tarquin had his arms firmly around Ress. She sat in front of him on the saddle, reeling from pain, and when they reached the wood elves capital of Menelwyn, the prince carried her to a house of healing. The elves, dressed in long white robes, looked her over and assured him that she was in perfect care. He kissed her head and whispered in her ear before mounting his horse and riding hard to the royal palace.

He took the steps there two at a time and called out to the guards to ask where Eldahir might be. He found his dear friend with his generals, looking over maps of the great swamp to the south.

The prince, gasping for breath, his arm held tightly to his rib cage, had burst through the door to a startled audience before he was able to muster as dignified a manner as he could. He explained to them all what had happened and several of the generals sprinted from the room calling for their horses and soldiers. Tarquin and Eldahir exited the palace and headed for the healers to check on Ress.

Eldahir noticed the grimace on his friend's face and the way he held his arm close to his ribs.

"Our healers can take the pain away from your broken ribs," Eldahir said.

Tarquin looked bemused.

"Have you yourself become a healer to so diagnose my injuries?"

The elf laughed.

"Nay, but I have seen too many soldiers bearing such injuries not to know what ails you."

They reached the house of healing and the head cleric met them at the door.

"Your fiancée can't have any visitors at this time," he told them. "She has lost a lot of blood and we placed her in a deep sleep to allow our poultices to work on her."

The healer took one look at Eldahir's friend and added, "Come with me, Prince Tarquin, and we will see about those ribs."

"You better go," Eldahir said, laughing, "or the father will have his apprentices bind and drag you into one of the healing rooms."

Tarquin was led to a bare room with only one bed and was pushed down upon it. Several clerics came and went, examining his ribs, much to Tarquin's dislike. They quickly brought back a potion and explained that it would take the pain away.

He swallowed it down and found quick relief while they tightly bound his torso.

•   •   •   •   •

Morganna the dark elf who had been transformed into a wood elf by the dwarvan god Dolgar was soon to be married or so she hoped. Her mind was set that Eldahir a true wood elf would propose. At least that was what her dear friend Ress had implied. She sat by a fountain one of many located in Menelwyn and thought of her family. Her father Tibersu the leader of the dark elves would be furious with her for marrying a wood elf a black mark on his family's reputation. Morganna knew that at some point she would have to face her father which would most likely end in a battle to the death.

She still held out hope for her brother, Boltrein. Morganna and he had shared a tight bond of familial love while growing up in the lightless underworld. They had run amok through capital and explored the dangerous caves and passages close to the city. She still loved him but had witnessed his turning firsthand by her father before escaping the vampire's grasp.

Boltrein had been her closest confidant and ally in a city of deceit and lies. Morganna held out a slim hope that he would still recall the love they shared before he had been turned.

•   •   •   •   •

Arantir and Trimimar, newly promoted captains in the elven cavalry and now stationed at the capital, were startled when bugle calls echoed from the palace.

The two quickly strapped on their swords, ran to the stables and found their horses already saddled by their soldiers. The elves quickly formed up fifty horsemen in exact lines and rode in columns of twos toward the palace.

Arantir and Trimimar worried that the capital was under attack and they shouted nervously back and forth to each other as their horses thundered down the grass lined streets. The last thing either one wanted was to fail in his duty as a new commander.

They were met by the palace guards who were formed into ranks in front of the steps of the elven palace.

General Orthorion walked down the palace steps and the horsemen lined up behind the foot soldiers with the two new captains readily accessible to the general should they be needed. Orthorion walked past the lines of elves directly toward Arantir and Trimimar.

Trimimar looked over at his friend.

"I wonder what this is about?" he asked.

"Looks like an ant hill has been knocked over," Arantir replied.

The general stopped before them.

"Large white orcs have attacked Prince Tarquin by the waterfall, not a league from our city," the general said bluntly. "Follow them and stop at nothing to eliminate the foul beasts that have soiled our homeland. And see if you can find out more about a woman called the black witch."

Orthorion then turned to address his foot soldiers.

The two captains, worried about what was to come, motioned to their soldiers to follow them out through the city gate. They went quickly to the waterfall and found the site where Prince Tarquin had engaged the strange orcs. The two captains dismounted, and their soldiers set up watching for the enemies.

Arantir and Trimimar quickly discovered where the orcs had crushed the underbrush in the attack. Arantir pointed down the track and gave an order to five of the elves.

"See where that goes and report back."

The elves rode off down the trail and Trimimar examined one of the dead orcs, using his boot to turn the beast over. Arantir approached him.

"Eight feet or I'm a goblin," Trimimar said. "Never seen a white one either."

Arantir pointed at one of the other corpses.

"Strange…but protective armor. I don't know what we are dealing with. Orcs from south of the escarpment? Difficult to say."

The elves sent to track the orcs reemerged from the brush then and their veteran sergeant pointed back up the path.

"It connects to one of the southern trails. There can't be many of them, from the look of the horses' passage."

Both the captains took their reins from a soldier and mounted up.

Arantir pointed to the track.

"Two scouts lead the way. We'll catch up to these orcs later today."

•   •   •   •   •

Tibersu, the undead lord of the Illanni came to his home for one last time to gather certain magical items from his study. He placed them all in an old leather bag and then steepled his hands before him and concentrated.

There wasn't a book or document in the room which he hadn't memorized, yet something still niggled at the edge of his mind. Following an urging he did not understand, he softly lay his head on the desktop and closed his eyes. He knew instantly that he was somewhere else.

It was a place with strange vibrations to it, and he sent out invisible mental tendrils to feel out these new surroundings and search the area. He suddenly encountered a powerful shield, a force unlike anything he had ever reckoned with, even that of Taza.

His eyes snapped open and he found himself lying on a plush rug. A female voice called out to him.

"Wake, Tibersu, my child."

He opened his eyes and slowly got to his feet. Sitting on a large throne before him was the most beautiful dark elf he had ever seen. The power that emanated from this being assured him that he was in front of his goddess, Adois, who could appear in any form she wanted. In Tibersu's mind, there was no question about who or what she was.

He bowed deeply, showing her great respect, something Taza never had never done.

"My lady. It is a wonder that I now stand here in your presence."

She laughed, her voice rich and low.

"You please me. My other pet, Taza, was not as politic as you, dear Tibersu, Lord of the Illanni."

Tibersu looked around the room at all the beautiful objects made of solid gold. The splendor before him was overwhelming.

"Taza failed due to his own desires and machinations," Tibersu said. "I have none...except to further empower my race to its former glory in preparation for when we live above ground once more."

An eerie chuckle came from the goddess.

"You will resume my plan," she said. "My brother must not have his peace on this planet Muiria. My children shall prevail, and it is through you that my plans will continue."

"As you wish," Tibersu responded. "I loath to say it, but I am not as powerful as Taza was when he ruled."

The goddess leaned forward, close to him and gave him a taste of her seductive power. Even though he was a vampire and could control his yearnings, a base desire he hadn't felt in eons washed over his body and mind.

"I know of such power that you could make use of in the near future," she said in a low husky voice. "This power will not corrupt...as did my staff. Here. I will make an etching in your mind of the place where you can find it."

She closed her eyes and Tibersu mentally watched in awe as a map appeared before him, but it was immediately followed by a searing pain in his head. He gasped and grabbed his skull with both hands.

"With this map ingrained in your mind, you will remember the location of the treasure," Adois told him. "Go forth and spread our power over Muiria. Time means nothing to you and me, but failure to uphold our bargain will elicit another visit from me and I guarantee it will not be as pleasurable as this one."

In a blink of an eye Tibersu was back in his study.

He glanced at his ancient time piece and saw that not a single grain of sand had dropped through it. It was as though time had come to a standstill while he was gone, but recalling the words of his goddess, he could still see the map etched in his mind. He knew it was a map that led to unstoppable power that would be his to further the cause of creating a world where vampires ruled. He smiled. How wonderful to have the goddess Adois walk with him on his mission to further vampirism.

He glanced out the window. If only she could change the yellow sun to one more conducive to vampires, he thought. Then he laughed.

"Who knows? Maybe she could."

White orcs broke through the edge of the forest and found the river. Aminol was just ahead of them.

The commander motioned to the twenty orcs remaining from the raid to go forward and they continued onward, knowing the elves would have sent a patrol after them. Night had now fallen on the day of their early morning attack on the prince, and the orcs slowed to rest their horses after they crossed the river.

They did not see the elven horsemen exit the forest and silently ride toward the river that marked the edge of the elven realm.

Using silent hand signals, the two new captains had pointed out their prey as they crossed over a hill and disappeared. Trimimar gave a signal and the column continued onward at a slower pace to ease the weariness of their horses. The ageless elves themselves were tireless to a point, but their mounts suffered from fatigue, as all animals and mortals did.

A scout had been sent ahead earlier to closely follow the retreating orcs. His mission was to do so without being seen or captured and now he rode back to his captains to report.

"There are twenty orcs ahead of us," he said to Arantir and Trimimar. "They take no care with their tracks and have only two orcs riding as rear guards some hundred paces behind the main group."

The scout saluted and rode back the way he had come. The company and its ever-anxious captains followed. They dared not fail to accomplish their first mission.

CHAPTER THREE

Eldahir, Morganna and Tarquin sat at Ress's bedside, talking softly, the day after the attack. The healers would not allow her to move around for still another day because the cut had been so deep. Tarquin and Eldahir were discussing the intrusion by the western orcs, and what they needed to do to investigate the one who had sent them, the black witch. When their conversation was finished, Tarquin reached out and held his love's hand.

"As soon as you're better, we'll be married," Tarquin said with a smile.

"I can't wait," Ress said, smiling back. "It seems as though we have been engaged forever, though I know it really hasn't been that long."

Seeing how much her friends were in love, Morganna sighed happily and glanced at Eldahir,

"So, my friend," Tarquin began, half teasing and half serious. "I believe there was something you wanted to do. At least, that's what you told me yesterday."

"I did, didn't I? Tell you, that is," Eldahir said.

Ress giggled.

"Yes, you did," she said and winked at Morganna.

Suddenly and awkwardly, Eldahir slipped out of his chair and knelt before Morganna. Reaching into his pocket he pulled out a small box and opened the lid. A matched set of wide, rose gold wedding rings etched with flowers and leaves lay inside.

Looking into her eyes, he suddenly found himself tongue-tied, and in a very un-elf-like manner, he opened his mouth and stuttered on his first word.

"Mor…Morganna, you are the love of my life, my true heart, my soul mate. I would be honored and pleased beyond measure if you would consent to become my wife."

Morganna beamed and blushed prettily as she reached out to take his hands in hers.

"Yes, Eldahir. Oh, yes, I, too, would be honored and happy beyond belief to have you for my spouse and life mate."

Eldahir grinned from ear-to-ear. He rose to his feet, bringing Morganna up with him, and the couple kissed and embraced each other. Ress sat up in bed, despite her tightly wrapped bandages, and shouted what both women were thinking.

"We can have a double wedding here in the forest!"

They were hushed by the healers around them who now had to bow their heads slightly to hide the brilliant smiles on their faces.

Tarquin spoke before thinking.

"What if it rains?"

Both women looked at him like he was an errant, outspoken child.

Tarquin quickly closed his mouth. The most important day of their lives was in the making. Obviously, his manly thoughts were not needed.

●   ●   ●   ●   ●

Tibersu had sent word for Martish to come to the Temple of Adois so he could inform her about the goddess's new mission.

Martish feared he might have underlying motives and she wracked her brain for a way to escape if he should try to turn her. An acolyte, wearing a long red robe with a mace at his waist, met her at the top of the first flight of steps and led her through a maze-like passageway. Martish memorized the route, but she sensed there were many guards posted throughout the maze, and it was probably also manned by vampires. The journey seemed to take far too long.

The acolyte finally came to a steep staircase, a full forty feet across, under a space that seemed to rise into the darkness above. Although her eyes were used to the darkness of the underworld, Martish could not see the ceiling of the chamber.

"Follow me. Lord Tibersu is waiting above," the acolyte informed her.

Nervously, she ascended the stairs that ended at a landing in front of two huge double doors. Martish doubted she could open them without help, but as she stepped onto the landing, the doors silently, magically opened on their own.

Leaving the acolyte at the landing, Martish entered the room alone and found Tibersu. She remembered how Illanni mothers had used his name to frighten their children.

The leader of the Illanni turned to her.

"Come, dear Martish. I won't bite. At least not this time," he said and chuckled.

Martish smiled at his subtle joke, but knew it was also a future warning. Her hand never strayed from her sword.

"You have summoned me, my lord?" she said.

"I have," Tibersu confirmed. "Because of your success against the cursed high elves, I have another mission for you. Come here to my table."

She approached and saw a well-drawn map spread out and held down at each corner by small bags of sand.

"This is a map given to me by our goddess. I want you to follow it to its end. There you will find treasure beyond measure. Bring everything you find back to me. You and your compatriots may keep the gold, but the magical artifacts are to be brought back for my exclusive use as the goddess has only given them to me. If you decide to escape with the treasure, I will find you and make you suffer a pain the likes of which you have never endured. Then I will kill you."

"What do these things of power look like? How will I know what to claim for you?"

"You will be able to feel the power within them," Tibersu said. "Such power cannot be controlled by one such as you. If you tried to use it, it would utterly destroy you. Only a warlock vampire such as myself could ever hope to wield it."

Tibersu had no idea if his words were true or not. Adois had told him just the opposite, but remembering what her staff had done to Taza, he didn't trust her promise. He did believe, though, that a non-magical person would probably find the item or items useless.

Martish nodded and examined the map. She looked up sharply at Tibersu.

"This will take us westward on the ocean to lands unknown to all but a few. How do I find a sea captain willing to embark on such a suicide mission?"

"I have already commissioned a ship and a knowledgeable captain," the vampire assured her. "He trades regularly in the west and will be paid handsomely. You have traveled in the land of light before. Take the best of your soldiers, find this treasure, and bring it back to me."

"How am I to know this captain?" Martish asked.

Tibersu grinned, showing his fangs.

"He will find you. Do not worry."

"As you wish, my lord," Martish said and rolled up the map.

She hurried out of the room, met the same acolyte at the landing and she ran past him down the stairs. Keeping up with her fast pace, Tibersu's minion then motioned her to follow him and soon they were outside the temple.

She breathed a deep sigh of relief. She had met alone with Tibersu and had lived to tell the tale.

The acolyte handed her a large purse containing the coins she would need for the mission.

•　　　•　　　•　　　•　　　•

At that time Boltrein was ensconced in his plain room in his family's huge manor house. His own spies had told him of the pending wedding of his sister Morganna and a filthy wood elf. He was furious. What was his sister doing?

First his father had given up ruling the manor and assumed the role as the dark elves' ruler and now this. He was sure to bare the brunt of the slight. The whole of the city would think that he and his clan had turned against them. Perhaps his spies had it wrong, but he was sure his father would hold him responsible. Boltrein instantly thought of his home. He would need more guards, but against his father a whole army of guards could not slow the forces of evil down.

He was suddenly alarmed "forces of evil" did he really consider his clan evil and not include himself. What if his sister had been right all along and it was right in front of his face? He would have to ponder more on this.

•　　　•　　　•　　　•　　　•

After Martish had left Tibersu, an Illanni with a fanged smile stepped out of the shadows and entered the temple. He reached the room she had just left in seconds.

"So, your plans are proceeding as you expected?" he asked.

Tibersu motioned the other vampire to a chair.

"The plans are progressing well, Ribald. Now, for your part, I am unleashing you and your cadre upon the world. Go forth and turn as many above-worlders as you can. They will make up the bulk of our army for the world above. Their loss will be meaningless. It will save the rest of us, as well as the regular Illanni, for the more important task of ruling...once the war is over."

Ribald smiled.

"My vampires are ready. We shall venture forth as soon as the sun is down and then go our separate ways and spread our dream over the surface world."

Tibersu felt elated. His machinations were coming true. Soon there would be enough vampires to pose a true threat to the world above and bring the dogs of light to heel.

•   •   •   •   •

Cyra the black witch knew that those who had destroyed Taza had future plans that would also be a threat to her. Using a powerful scrying spell, she then located the ones she had seen during the fight at the tower on Dragon Isle.

Next she called for her right-hand man and confidant, Talchic.

The warlock Melgor, now living under the name Talchic, came as fast as he could. The sound of his staff echoed off the marble flooring and when he reached Cyra's room, he held his staff under what remained of his right arm. He had lost the rest of it many months earlier in a battle with two warlocks and two sorceresses.

He opened the door with his left hand and bowed.

"Mistress called?" he asked.

Cyra smiled at her trusted counselor.

"I have located the ones who killed Taza," she said. "They are in Menelwyn. I have already dispatched a company of my orcs to kill as many as possible."

Talchic looked concerned.

"They are strong opponents," he said, "and might easily dispatch those you sent. Revealing yourself at this time might not be wise, mistress. They are headstrong and determined. They might follow the orcs back here...or capture some of them and extract more knowledge about your existence and about where you reside. I urge caution."

The sorceress nodded.

"Perhaps you are right. I might have reacted too soon. I have also learned that some Illanni are seeking a ship to sail west in search of treasure."

"How can you ferret out such information?" the one-armed warlock asked. She laughed heartily.

"You have your sources. I have mine, even in the vile city of Illan. I'm sending a larger company of my white orcs to chase them down and stop their meddling. It must be important for the Illanni if they're willing to leave their deep holes to sail west."

•   •   •   •   •

The elven horsemen closed on their prey, and two of them slipped down into the thigh high grass. Stringing their bows, they darted off into the darkness, picking up speed as they ran. It was time to attack. Morning was almost upon them. The orcs, tired from riding all night, would be at their worst.

The two orcs who were riding rearguard paid little attention to their surroundings. They neither listened nor looked behind to see if they were being followed. One of these white orcs had even fallen asleep in its saddle.

The two elves ran past their forward scout and notched arrows in their bows. Slipping up on the orcs had taken no effort at all and from out of the darkness, their arrows flew straight and true. They fired off a second volley, but the orcs had already died and slid off their horses.

The elves quickly closed the distance and took control of the orc's horses. Exhausted by their retreat, the steeds were relieved when the elves took their reins. The weight of the orcs had been a heavy burden on the beasts.

The remaining elves formed a tight line with their lances lowered. Gently urging their horses forward with their heels, they advanced, overtaking their scout and two bowmen while they moved forward as quietly as possible. The scout and the two bowmen followed the line and when the horsemen were close enough, one elf sounded the charge.

The white orcs were caught by surprise as the elves rode directly into them. Chaos ensued as the two forces intermingled. The huge orcs made easy targets for the elven lances that pierced their skin and knocked those mounted from their horses. Many of the orcs were dismounted, preferring to fight on foot, and even on the ground they stood taller than the slender elven horses and they could easily grab a rider from his saddle.

The fighting turned fierce. The elves outnumbered the orcs, but the orcs' strength and size gave them the edge. Still, many of the elves rode circles around the orcs and peppered them with arrows until they fell, mortally wounded. As the sun rose over the Mordolwyn mountains, half the orcs had already fallen as Trimimar led yet another charge into their ranks.

His friend Arantir was fighting on foot and was battered to the ground by an orc wielding a huge sword.

Seeing the predicament his fellow captain was in, Trimimar charged into the melee himself and maneuvered his horse to the attack, but the orc saw him coming. Taking a wild strike, the white orc forced Arantir to lay flat on the ground and turned to grab the bridle of Trimimar's charging horse. The mount was brought to a stop by the mighty power of the giant orc, but it reared up and its front hooves flailed the air and struck the orc about the head.

Trimimar was almost thrown from his saddle, but he quickly regained his balance. Gripping his lance, he drove it deep into the orc's eye, but his enemy's face showed only surprise before toppling over and dragging the captain's lance with him.

Trimimar drew his sword and surveyed the battlefield. Every orc was down, and the elves were now riding through them and driving their lances and swords into the bodies to make sure they were dead.

Arantir stood up and called out.

"Leave one alive. We must question it."

Several elves, their swords still drawn, led a limping orc over to the two captains. The two commanders looked it over and noticed only one deep wound in its leg where a lance point stuck out the back of its thigh.

"Where do you come from?" Trimimar asked it.

The orc laughed at him but answered.

"We come from the west, but that is all I will tell you." The elf cocked his head.

"Who sent you here to spoil our sacred land? Speak now, and I may spare your life."

The orc stopped laughing and turned serious. He seemed uncertain if the pointy-eared enemy spoke the truth or not. He decided to take a chance.

"The black witch."

The orc then whipped around and knocked the two guards to the ground before jumping at Arantir. The elf was faster and with a single swipe of his sword, the treacherous orc's head fell to the ground and rolled. Its body remained upright a moment longer with blood spurting from its neck as its heartbeat for the last time.

Looking around, the captains saw that ten of their soldiers were badly wounded and others suffered from varying degrees of lesser injuries. A cleric who rode with them saw to the more seriously wounded and wrapped them in their cloaks and placed them on horses. Those who suffered only minor injuries wrapped their injuries up and mounted up.

It was time to turn north and ride home to the sacred forest of Ravannhiel.

The new captains were unhappy that so many of their fellow elves had been wounded, and they wondered if the legendary General Orthorion would still be pleased that they had accomplished their goal.

They truly hoped so.

CHAPTER FOUR

It took dark elf Martish time to decide which twenty Illanni to take from her company because their numbers were so reduced by the battle with the high elves. She had lost many of her most trusted followers. In the end, she chose those that had been in her service the longest and she included the company's warlock and healer. These she could trust to a point.

Strapping on their protective leather armor and donning their voluminous cloaks, the twenty left the dark of the underworld for the sun-bright world above.

It took her company of soldiers a week of hard riding on the rolling terrain to reach what was considered the west. They traversed the tall grass covered plains, the foliage reaching up to their horse's chests, and eventually they made it to the forested west coast. Following the map, Martish found the city of Trudoc on the western ocean.

As they approached the city, a giant white orc waited silently in the waving grass and then sprinted off to find the black witch as the Illanni passed.

$$\bullet \qquad \bullet \qquad \bullet \qquad \bullet$$

The company of twenty dark elves rode through the streets of Trudoc which reminded each of them of the slums of Illan. The streets were full of trash and there were open sewers running down the sides of the street.

Martish led the way down towards the ocean and she could see the masts of dozens of ships out on the water. There were strange birds, flying above her, all around the sky, and they also caught her eye. The city itself contained people of all races, orcs and their ilk included and she saw the giant white orcs and considered that they could pose a problem in a fight. They finally reached the docks and found hundreds of ships of all different sizes moored to the docks or anchored offshore.

Martish ordered her soldiers to remain mounted and she got off her horse and slowly made her way to the edge of the dock. She had been raised in the deep places of the world and was used to the crystal-clear water there. The bay in front of her looked filthy and she could see a dead body, bloated and swollen, floating amongst the flotsam.

She had been standing there for several minutes watching the boats and the garbage filled bay when she felt a man approaching her back. She turned quickly and saw a crusty old captain walking toward her.

When he was near enough, he bowed.

"I'm captain Rudolf of the ship Swift Wind," he said to her. "I believe a lord Tibersu has arranged for me to take you west."

She nodded her head without speaking, she did not want to give her accent away in such a public place.

"Have your company follow and I will lead you to my ship," Rudolf said.

The captain blew his nose once with a dirty handkerchief, turned and began walking.

Martish and her company followed and wove their way past the ships' loads that were stacked high, by the stevedores and the crowded warehouses. Finally, they reached the Swift Wind.

Martish walked behind the captain up the gang plank and was amazed to see such a clean ship, compared to Rudolf himself and his disheveled appearance. Every rope was perfectly stowed away and all the paint shined. She could tell that it had just been freshly applied.

The crew looked equally as disreputable as their captain, though and they ran a large gangway out—probably otherwise used to haul off goods—for her soldiers to walk their horses up as they came aboard.

The captain approached her.

"We have rigged up stables below. It might be crowded for them, but it will do in a pinch."

Martish finally spoke and her voice had the lilt of an Illanni, but she hoped the captain could not tell.

"My men will take care of their horses. Your sailors need not worry about them."

Rudolf, now acting as a gentleman, escorted her down narrow stairs to the deck below.

"I know it's not much," he said, "but here is your cabin."

It was small to say the least and once inside she could barely stand upright. Her few belongings could be stowed away in netting attached to the walls.

Her soldiers settled into the ship below deck. They would sleep in hammocks like the sailors who manned the Swift Wind.

The ship sailed on the morning tide and Martish walked the deck watching the well-trained crew as the boat made its way out of the harbor. She was impressed with how well trained the crew was and watched as they crawled through the rigging or handled the ropes on the deck of the ship. She also noted the many barrels that were filled with weapons and set about the deck.

The western sea crossing was a calm one except for one small storm that rose up from the southwest and upset the horses below deck more than the passengers.

Martish, the dark elf, looked out across the endless sea in fascination. She had thought the lands she had traveled seemed endless, but here, in the mist of this vast sea, Martish was speechless.

During their voyage the sailors and the passengers had not mingled, and the strange language and the weapons of the dark ones had put the crew ill at ease. Then, on one clear day, a sailor high up in the crow's nest cried "Land Ho!" and his call was the one that the dark ones and the sailors alike had greatly anticipated.

Martish joined the captain,

"Do you know of a port nearby?" she asked.

"Aye, but the city guards would not be pleased with an armed party landing at their docks."

Before she could reply, Rudolf quickly added, "But don't worry. There is a cove used by pirates and smugglers just north of the city. The king turns a blind eye to the trading of goods that take place there so he can avert any attack on the city as retribution for his interference. I have used it many times. It should do just fine."

Wondering if Rudolf's ship was a pirate or a smuggler, Martish went to her birth and unrolled the map. There was no marking for the city on the map and the surrounding shoreline was indistinct.

She would have to question the locals, and she knew that could cause trouble and might even reveal who they really were, that is if the Illanni were known in this land. Still, she would have to risk it.

She took the map to the captain and laid it out in front of him on a barrel head. Martish motioned for the captain to study the document.

"Have you seen or heard of a mountain range near to your cove?" she asked.

The captain humphed and hawed before speaking.

"I have heard of such a place, but I never have traveled so far inland. There is a little used trail that leads through the jungle inland. If there are mountains, they will be there."

Several turns of the clock later the captain changed direction with the favorable wind and steered the ship straight towards the shore.

Martish was worried the captain was touched in the head and she joined him.

"Are we grounding the ship?" she asked.

He laughed.

"Nay, fair lady. See the breakers? That's the outflow from the river emptying into the ocean."

Just as he said, the ship rocked a little, but bore down on the estuary without incident. Martish watched as a small cove opened up with ships anchored on either side of the river. Several roads led off in all directions from the riverbanks into the thick palms and underbrush.

"I've been mulling over the map that you showed me," Rudolf said to Martish. "The only mountains that I have heard about should lie down yond middle track. That one should take you to a land of flat ground that'll be perfect for your horses."

She turned toward him, and her hand gripped her sword's pommel and she spoke in a stern voice.

"Why have you withheld this information from me?"

"I simply wanted to stay alive. I guessed who you were as soon as your soldiers led their horses on to the ship. I figured that if I told you where the mountains were, you'd slit our throats in the middle of the night and continue on by yourselves."

Martish just ground her teeth in frustration before she spoke again.

"I might just be tempted to do that right now, but I'm sure the sailors from these other ships might take offense."

She turned away and barked the command to unload the horses.

• • • • •

The vampire Ribald, after he had been ordered to go above ground and spread vampirism, sprinted up out of the temple. His plan would finally be put into play.

Fifty vampires waited for him in the cave that led to the outside world. He was sure fifty was enough after he had accounted for casualties. Some of his cadre might be caught out in the sun, some might be killed by their prey and one or two might even disobey his orders to escape the Illanni's reputed battle prowess.

Ribald reached the cave and addressed the vampires gathered there.

"Tibersu has given us the order. We are to move out after sundown."

The vampires all smiled, showing their teeth and grasping each another's shoulders. This was the day they had been training for and they were ready to venture forth into the lands of the living.

Blood would be spilled in the near future and they would satiate their thirst.

• • • • •

One turn of the clock later Martish's company was riding down a small sandy trail in stifling hot conditions. Even the trees above them failed to keep the sun's heat away. Martish's veterans of the surface world had never encountered heat this draining, but her soldiers knew not to complain or they would face the whip or even death. Their commander was a hard woman.

These twenty soldiers had ridden for hundreds of years with her and knew better than anyone what she was capable of if riled.

Early the following day they exited the forest and looked out over a plain of twisted trees and endless thorns bushes. There was no grassland that had been promised by the ship's captain. Seething inside, Martish studied the land and the path they had ridden on. It forked, one branch going south and one north, and she took out the map and studied it.

There was no indication on it of the paths or even of the plain. She rolled up the map and slapped it against her horse.

"Damn Tibersu," she whispered. Was there no person she could query in this Adois bespoken wasteland?

Martish turned to her soldiers, a grimace on her face.

"We go north," she commanded.

She wished she had the eyesight of her cousins, the wood elves or the high elves, but years underground denied her that power. For now she headed in the direction she thought might lead her to the mountains.

Her company had been on the road two more days when Martish heard horns sounding from the dense jungle to the right of the road.

Suddenly the large white orcs she had seen in the crowds of Trudoc vaulted out of the jungle. They were all white in color and almost as tall as her soldiers, even when mounted.

Her dark elves dropped their cloaks, drew their weapons immediately and charged into their attackers without a command.

Their superior weapon skill gave them a slight advantage and several of the orcs fell immediately. The orcs could easily reach up and pull the riders off their horses, but then Martish's warlock joined the battle. Spells of fire struck the orcs like darts and could not be put out.

Despite their wounds, the orcs fought on and showed far more élan than any regular orc. These were well trained soldiers, Martish realized, and on a mission to stop her.

Several of her dark elves had gone down and Martish struck left and right with her sword, severing arms and heads, as she rode into the most intense fighting.

She saw and then felt the heat of a fireball spell. Martish looked up the road and watched a troop of the large orcs be disintegrated by the spell. If they had joined the fight, she knew, the dark elves would all have died in this cursed place.

She turned her attention back to the skirmish and spotted the leader of the orcs standing tall and shouting his soldiers onwards. Martish rode directly at the beast and swung her sword, but the orc struck it aside, numbing her arm in the process.

She pulled hard on the reins of horse and her mount flailed its two front legs. One hoof caught the white orc commander in the face and he fell backward.

Martish attacked immediately. The orc raised his sword, but she struck first and cleaved its arm at the wrist, cutting the orc's hand off.

As his sword fell to the ground, he vaulted into the jungle, holding his severed arm and calling to his fellow orcs. Soon what was left of them and their wounded captain were scared off by the last of the spells. The orcs jumped into the jungle and disappeared into its dark depths.

Martish rode around the company and watched her healer seeing to the wounded. She saw that three would no longer rise and she shouted out.

"See to the dead and bring their belongings along." She whipped her horse around and asked those on the ground, "Who were those overgrown things?"

"I had heard of giant orcs, but thought it a myth till we reached Trudoc," one of her soldiers said as he wiped the sweat from his face.

Martish rode up to him and hitting him hard on the side of the head with her fist.

"If any of you have any more myths," she said, "you'd better tell me now or you'll end up as dead as those three."

She pointed at the offending soldier.

"I need you or I'd run you through right now," she said to him.

●   ●   ●

Martish and her company had been riding for a week without having seen anyone other than the orcs that had attacked them when one of her scouts came riding back and called out to her.

"Mistress! Look to the horizon."

She squinted her eyes and looked where the soldier pointed. Sure enough, on the horizon were dark objects that looked to be mountains. Martish was loathe to enter the wasteland now between her and the distant mountains, she knew she must go on. If the map were right, there would be what looked to be a natural spring that turned into a small river halfway across and she hoped that they would eventually be able continue through the heat and the sun and reach that spot.

The wasteland was dry and barren of any life except brittle grass and stunted trees. With each of their horses' steps, the hooves threw up a cloud of dry dust and left a telltale sign of their passing. The dust soon drifted up into the air and coated the horses and her troops.

The company struggled through this vast hell and kept the mountains in their sight, but on the fifth day they ran out of water. Unused to the heat and without nourishing water, her soldiers continued onward, slunk down in their saddles. The three horses that carrying their provisions stumbled along slowly behind the column of exhausted warriors.

Finally, Martish thought she saw the welcome sight of greenery and she called to her soldiers.

"Come now! It is but a little way. I can make out trees in the distance and that means water."

The dark ones woke from their heat induced lethargy and soon the whole company, including their mounts, were drinking fresh water that bubbled out of the ground and turned the once dry rock bed into a stream.

After a half turn of the clock at the freshwater stream, her horses and her troop refreshed and the water skins filled, Martish ordered her soldiers to mount up and ride.

As one of the soldiers mounted, she heard a cry of pain and she whipped around in her saddle, her sword drawn. A soldier was writhing in pain on the ground. She steered her horse over to him while the rest of her company stared outward looking any signs of danger. Still seated on her horse, Martish saw out the corner of her eye a long snake slithering away.

She called to the injured dark one.

"Mount up, you fool! Secura can heal you."

The dark elf did not move. Martish dismounted and kicked the body over. Her warrior was dead. Great boils covered his face and his tongue was swollen and protruding from his mouth.

Martish turned to the others.

"Make this a lesson. We are in a strange land and anything here can be dangerous and can kill us."

She consulted her map. The stream flowed straight westward towards the mountains.

"Come," she said, "Bring the horse and whatever is of use from this corpse."

● ● ● ● ●

The stream ran westward and soon the beginning of a small forest appeared. Its trees grew greater in height the further west they went and blocked the devilish sun, but the miserable heat still followed them.

In the distance they saw their goal, the beckoning mountains. Huge black rocks thrust up from the ground and made a formidable mountain chain. Martish could tell the mountains were relatively new as there was barely any erosion showing.

They began following game trails along the course of the river, but many times had to dismount and lead their horses forward through the thickening forest. They continued to venture onward toward the craggy mountains.

When Martish and her company reached the start of the foothills of the mountains, she looked at the map again and saw it clearly showed a trailhead that led well into the mountainous range to a more vaguely depicted cave. What was in the cave worried her for a single click of the clock, but she wiped that thought from her mind. Whatever awaited them, she and her company were more than a match.

As they cut their way through the underbrush, Martish began to think that the map had once again led then astray, but the map was true to the knowledge of its cartographer. It did take several days of combing along the foothills for her company to find a path made of dangerous gravel. The rough surface was capable of breaking the leg of a horse as it led up into the mountains, but at least as they gained altitude, a steady breeze cut across the path and cooled them off.

The trail meandered along through the mountains, always on a bed of black rocks, but eventually they reached a glade. The horses could go no further, but there was plenty of forage for them to eat. One narrow path, too small for the horses, led upwards from the valley floor and switched back and forth until, high up, it turned and disappeared from sight.

Martish sat on her horse and quickly made up her mind. She pointed at the grass-covered glade and at the spoke to a pair of her soldiers.

"You two will stay here and watch the horses and guard the path that brought us here. The rest of you, stake your horses out and follow me."

The dark ones were all used to the narrow paths of the underworld and they quickly took off on the trail without a care in the world, lightly treading their way upwards into the mountains. The company walked the dangerous path for seven days and nights before they reached the end of their journey.

In front of Martish and her company, the trail ended at a dark opening in the cliff wall.

It didn't look like much and it could easily have been overlooked. Considering how excited Tibersu had been over the map, Martish thought, this passage was rather mundane. She had expected a great carved entryway. This was a mere fissure in the wall and her dark elf company would have to slither sideways to get through.

Martish did not know how long they had been walking in the slit—a full turn of the clock maybe—when suddenly it opened up into a normal cave like the ones the dark ones were familiar with in their own underground world. As they all stepped out into the first large room, several of her soldiers automatically went to the next opening to act as guards. They peered into the darkness and their eyes, accustomed to the dark places of the world, posed no problem to them for seeing what lay ahead.

Martish scanned the room and noticed the sharp right angles to the corners. This was a delved room that had not seen a living thing for centuries. Long ago the portions of the ceiling must have fallen, possibly due to an earthquake and had given the floor the appearance of a rocky cave.

She went to the passage that led onwards into the mountains. One of the dark ones pointed to the floor and a pile of decayed wood,

"This was a carved doorway," he said. "and by what's left of the wood pile, it's been a long time since it has been used. There are no tracks disturbing what remains of it and none either that we can see further down the passage in the dust."

Martish put her hand on her soldier's shoulder and agreed with the Illanni. She turned to the others.

"Leave your heavy cloaks here," she commanded them, "just in case we can venture back to this place. 'Tis pointless to be burdened with them. We know not what lies ahead. Keep your senses alert. We are finally in our own element."

Her troops shared smiles between them. They were happy to be out of the sun and back in the coolness of caves.

She looked over her company and saw that they were eager to be off, but she had made another decision for them.

"We will eat now and rest here for the night. There is no telling when we will eat again. Also, I want alert soldiers at my back tomorrow, not ones who are rushing off into the darkness."

After sleeping amid the rubble and exchanging night guards twice, Martish awoke and stirred the others from their sleep. She motioned for them to continue onwards through the passage. It led them straight ahead, never deviating from its course, and was always hewn from the solid rock. They never saw any natural rock formations at all.

Martish heard water falling with her keen elven hearing and the noise grew in volume as they progressed. Soon they found a fissure in the side of the wall with pure mountain water flowing fast though it as it disappeared down a hole in the floor. The spray from it felt cool on the Illanni skin after their days of enduring the heat of this strange new world.

Martish looked at the rounded corners stone where the water flowed through the floor. A shifting of the chamber had apparently occurred a long time ago and she thought perhaps a movement of the stone had caused the stream to penetrate the room.

It was the first visible hint that the passage was as ancient as she had thought. She barked an order.

"Refill your water skins. There's no telling if we'll ever pass this way again."

CHAPTER FIVE

Several days later the dark ones were still trodding along the passage when suddenly the tunnel ended.

A huge cavern spread out before them and the company immediately drew their weapons and looked for signs of enemies, a trait they had honed in the darkness of the underworld they called home. There seemed to be nothing dangerous where they stood and Martish pointed to a set of steps zigzagging down to the cavern floor.

Two of the company immediately began descending the stairs without a verbal order from their leader.

One of the scouts returned and used hand signals to motion that the way was clear at the bottom of the steps. They proceeded down the steps, weapons still drawn, eyes scanning the length and breadth of the cavern. The steps ended at a carved pathway that continued out into the darkness. Weaving their way through a great cavern, they walked along the path until they reached the center of the cavern.

Suddenly roars erupted all around them and they found themselves under attack and surrounded.

"Dragon spawn!" yelled out one of the oldest and wisest of her company.

Martish had heard the legends of dragon spawn as a youngster when they were told by adults to little ones to scare them. The creatures supposedly looked like little man-sized dragons standing on two legs with razor-like claws they could use for lightning fast strikes. They were black in color and so could hide from most attackers, but they had never fought an illanni, it was said.

The darkness of the cavern this day was no friend for the dragon spawn, and the dark elves shot arrows into their ranks two times and felled many of them before the dragonets reached the dark Illanni company. The first line of the attackers pitched backward, arrows protruding from various parts of their bodies, and the wounded lay writhing in pain as the second wave jumped over them with their incredibly strong legs.

The Illanni fired again before being plowed over by the dragonets, but their attackers were quick and incredibly strong. Illanni swords flew this way and that, blocking the attackers' sharp claws and returning their killing blows to them. Several dark elves in the company spun backward to avoid the deep killing strikes from the claws of the enemy and the bites from their mouths, open now to show their numerous sharp teeth. Dark elf blood flew into the air as well along with the blood of the attackers.

Martish fought against two dragonets and kept them at bay with her darting sword work. One of them attacked her, its razor-like claws coming overhead and aiming for her face, but the Illanni officer quickly swung her sword upwards. Its sharp edge passed between two of the claws sliding downward toward her and sliced down through to one wrist and sheared off a goodly portion of the dragonet's hand.

Grasping its wound, the creature darted back into the dark cavern, but Martish still had to battle the second one. After dueling back and forth with the dragonet for a few clicks of the clock, she used her strong backhand and cut across the dragonet's chest. Her sword sliced through bone, sinew and heart.

All around her the company of dark elves fought for their lives. The dark ones' swords had a longer reach and gave them the advantage, but after the initial attacks, some of Martish's command started shooting arrows and picked off one dragonet after another. The other dark ones continued their individual duels with the dragonets in the utter darkness of the cavern. The dark ones' magic user started to light the cavern up with fire spells and these either injured or killed the dragonets and drove them all back. The last wave of attacking dragonets was struck down before they could reach the dark elves.

The combat continued on for some time until a mournful dragonet horn was blown and as suddenly as they had appeared, the dragonets were gone.

The dark elves drew deep breaths and kept scanning the darkness around them. The soldiers immediately took up defensive positions as they looked around for more attackers. Martish assessed the damage to her company.

In all, three had fallen in the attack and one still lay on the cavern floor and tried not to scream in pain after having had her stomach ripped out. Martish knelt by the wounded dark elf. She had served with Martish for several hundred years and was a vital member of the company.

Without any emotion on her face, Martish leaned over and slit the wounded woman's throat. The wounded dark elf expected no more from her leader. She would have died anyway in several days and she had expected her beloved captain to relieve her from any needless suffering.

Martish then stood and quietly issued her next command.

"Quickly take what we need. We should move out from this accursed place."

Once again they got back on the pathway and began walking along the same cut stone they had been following for days. They remained constantly on alert for more denizens of the cave, but no more appeared.

The path ended in a wide balcony that opened out over an immense cavern. Martish could neither see the roof nor the bottom despite all her years of living underground.

Suddenly she heard a clear, booming voice in her head,

"I welcome you to my tomb, Martish of Illan. I was told of your arrival. I can sense the evil that resides in your heart. That is a good thing. Otherwise I might feed you to my guardians, who I believe you have met and bested. Stupid little beings, but they do keep the riffraff out. But I was warned that you would visit, and I am remiss not to welcome you to my abode."

"Told by who?" Martish asked irritably. "I am supposed to be here in secret. To pick up valuables for my lord Tibersu. Why then were we attacked?"

The voice echoed up at her from the depths of the pit.

"So many questions. I tire of telepathy. You can't expect me to give away my treasure. I had to at least try and protect it by judging you and your warriors with my little ones."

There was a scraping sound and a giant dragon's head, dark as pitch, reared up in front of Martish and spoke.

"It was the goddess Adois who told me and she promised me certain things to improve the value of my horde of treasure."

Martish let her breath out. She had surprised the company around her who had never seen her so stupefied.

"There are no black dragons on Muiria," she said. "How come there is one living here now…unknown to the world?"

"That is a long story, young one," the black dragon answered. "When the dragons came to this place, I followed them, but the door to the void shut before

I was completely through. I left a tail and part of my wing in that cold nothingness. The other dragons were so enamored by this world, though, that I escaped notice. Arriving here, I fell and ended up in this cavern, the top covered by the rocks that I had fallen through and dislodged. I have existed since the beginning of this world, unable to fly, stuck in this cavern. If I tried to venture forth, the other dragons would surely kill me…although I would take down many of the attackers in such an epic battle."

"How do you survive, entombed in such place?" Martish asked. "These are young mountains, but your age alone is remarkable. Do you go by any name?"

The dragon huffed a few times and Martish realized that it was laughing.

"Small mortal, you are full of more questions? The simple answer is I simply love to sleep. There is nothing more to do here. The dragonets revere me as a god and bring me food and treasure. What more can a flightless dragon do? As for my name, to give it out might give my enemies power over me. As to the mountains, they are young, but they have shifted up against and around my home. I have placed an anti-aging spell on this cavern, quite a powerful spell. I have been forgotten by everything on Muiria."

Martish cared little for a tale of the life of a dragon and she got right to her point.

"I was sent here for weapons for me to return to my master. However, I was not told the sort of items he requires."

The dragon huffed again.

"In time. I have been promised healing and certain other items if you take these precious gifts to your ruler. But they are still precious to me. How can I trust you? You may take flight with my treasures."

Martish was worried that the encounter was not going the way she had worked it out in her head. She had heard that dragons were prone to chatter away for endless turns of the clock, but she needed quick answerers. The idle chitchat boded ill for a lifetime spent huddled in the cavern.

"I promise to take these treasures to my master," the dark elf said. "If not, my master would search for me. When I was found, I would be tortured and killed in an unimaginable way. There is nothing more I can do to appease you."

The dragon turned serious.

"Know you this. My commands come from a god with the evilest heart I have ever encountered. She has promised me healing and other things for my treasure, and I intend for it to be so. I will hold you to your word or I shall crawl forth from this hole and track you down myself."

The monstrous head dropped from view and suddenly, with a great spout of flame, the black dragon lit up a massive fire pit that was in the center of the cavern. All around the fire appeared gold and other precious items, and with several growls of differing pitch, the black dragon ordered the dragonets to gather various items from the massive mound of treasure.

Martish and several of her company standing by her inhaled deeply at what they saw before them, an entire lifetime of dragon treasure.

"Look!" one of her company said.

He pointed to the dark openings in the walls of the dragon chamber. Launching from them were winged dragonets—not unlike the ones the Illanni had just fought – that flew in circles and landed among the dragon's belongings amid a shower of gold.

They all quickly began searching through the items and every now and then one of the dragonets would bring an object to the black dragon. With the black dragon's approval, the items were then wrapped in black cloth and placed in a long narrow box.

In a turn of the clock, the quest was completed. All the while Martish and her company stood ready to repel any attack, even one from the black dragon itself.

Finally, two dragonets took hold of the handles of the long, delicately carved box and flew to the balcony. Warily they set it down in front of Martish before they flew quickly away.

The black dragon then raised its head level to the balcony and Martish stared into the depths of the darkest black eyes she had ever seen. She could now tell other Illanni that she had looked into the eyes of pure evil.

"Go now. Martish of the dark elves," the dragon said. "I see certain traits in you that I too have possessed in the past. I have grown rather docile in my old age."

Martish ordered two of her company to take up the decorated box, and the dark ones then slowly withdrew from the dragon's lair. All their eyes were focused on the dragon as they retreated.

Their way out was simple and they followed back along the passage they had entered. When they came across the ambush site, they found it had been picked clean by the remaining dragonets. They reached the final room of the passage and donned their heavy cloaks. Carrying the crate through the fissure proved difficult, but soon they were outside on a warm sunny day. They quickly began the walk back to their horses and the long journey home.

One night after they had ridden back across and out from the scorched plain, Martish was sitting by the fire when she was approached by one of her company.

"Mistress, we were wondering if the boat will still be waiting for us at the dock?" the Illanni asked her.

Martish smiled.

"It had better be. I tire of this intense heat. If it's not, by the way, I will search down that captain and skin him alive."

• • • • •

They needed not to worry for the ship was waiting for them in the cove. Martish waved to the captain and she gave her horse to another to load it onboard. She ran up the boarding ramp and was soon standing next to the Rudolf.

"Did the map prove accurate?" he asked.

She looked sideways at him and answered, "It provided enough details."

The captain saw that one of the horses had a long crate, covered by canvas, tied to its side and he smiled.

"Successful trip," he said.

Martish remained silent and the captain knew he had just overstepped his boundaries.

As soon as the ship's crew had released it from its moorings, the captain maneuvered it slowly out of the cove and the sea breezes fluffed out the sails. Once more they reached the sea, but the ship turned to head east this time.

The ship made good time and the captain explained to Martish that the southern wind gave them the extra headway.

• • • • •

It was several weeks till the ship sighted land again and as soon as the sailor in the crow's nest had shouted, "Land ho!" all hell broke loose on the ship.

The Illanni had gathered along the railing to see the oncoming land and each privately gave a prayer of thanks that they had made it across the sea.

Suddenly one of the dark illanni cried out and Martish saw the bloody end of a cutlass protruding from his chest.

"Ware!" Martish shouted.

Two sailors began swinging at her. She ducked one, drew a dagger from her boot and jammed it under his chin and up into his brain. She vaulted up onto a crate and quickly gave a look at her soldiers battling all around the ship.

She felt a searing pain in her leg as a thick crossbow bolt struck her in the right thigh. She dropped to one knee and drew her sword. Martish was quickly surrounded and she could barely keep the slashing cutlasses away from her. She neatly skewered one sailor and then saw another pitch forward with a long iron pike transfixing him. One of her soldiers had come to help her. Thankfully, she thought.

She was then momentarily free from the fighting and she reached down and pulled the crossbow bolt from her thigh. She screamed, but there was not even a tick of the clock to rest for the ship's captain was signaling her to single combat.

She leaped off the crate and landing in front of him. Her wounded thigh started to give way and she adjusted by taking more weight on her left leg.

Her opponent laughed.

"So, the mighty Illanni leader is hurt?" he said. "I'll be happy to confiscate that chest from you."

"Touch that and not only will you bring my wrath onto you, but the Goddess Adois as well," she responded.

Her threats bothered the pirate captain little and he began circling her. Martish began slowly circling too while her blood flowed freely down her leg.

Rudolf then attacked. Left, right, left, right, darted his thin epee. Martish blocked all the first blows, but then he struck out in a straight line toward her wounded leg. His sword penetrated her leather armor easily and she hopped backward, but as she retreated, the captain followed and kept striking out at her.

She parried each strike and then, with incredible speed and despite her wounds, she went on the offensive. She batted the captain's sword away and stabbed him in the shoulder. He tried desperately to regain the advantage when Martish dropped to her wounded knee and let out a loud grunt of pain. Her sword swept out in front of her and the captain danced out of the way. Next, she threw her dagger and it caught the captain in the face and hit his right eye as he turned his head.

Now blind in one eye, with his hand the captain put pressure on his now bleeding eye socket. He launched a desperate counterattack. Martish barely rolled away from him on the bloodied deck, but with great effort she stood, favoring her right leg greatly. The captain attacked, but as he approached her, the Illanni pivoted, swung her sword at the same time and caught the captain across the back of the neck. He fell, slowly dying.

The Illanni healer hurried to Martish's side and cast several spells on her leg before helping Martish up and lending her a shoulder for support. The remaining nine Illanni all bore some sign of being wounded.

Meanwhile, several dark ones had herded the remaining sailors to the side of the ship and were holding them at sword point.

Martish looked over the cowed and wounded seamen.

"You will get us to shore and live," she said. "Those who don't help will die now."

That more than motivated the crew to get in position and steer the ship towards shore. The bosun walked up to Martish,

"Do you want to head into port?" he asked.

The Illanni shook her head. "No, we ground the vessel. I don't doubt that afterward you'll be more than able to get this ship back to sea."

The man smiled. He was about to become the owner of the ship.

He ordered the main sails up and used only the topsails to slowly approach the beach. There was a sharp jolt as the ship's bow dug into the sand in the shallow water. Panicked sounds came from the horses below, but the sailors and the passengers were little troubled.

The Illanni unloaded the horses and their provisions and took special care with the long chest as they brought everything to shore.

The sailors then started rowing two longboats as mightily as they could with long lines from them attached back to the stern of the ship. It was imperative they get the ship off the sand before the low tide came.

The bosun expected several of the crew to challenge his right to the ship, his sword remained ready at his side for them.

CHAPTER SIX

An Illanni messenger raced up the stairs of the temple building. An acolyte in a blood-red robe met him and escorted him inside. He knew that the message might contain bad news, and his lord brooked no delays. Why else would a non-vampire be chosen to deliver the news to the ruler of the Illanni people?

The messenger took a deep breath before he entered the large temple room and handed the parchment to his lord. Tibersu quickly scanned the contents. The anger that filled the leader's heart—if he even had one, the messenger wondered—shot fires of rage through his veins, now bulging to the point that they were physically visible pulsating on the middle of his forehead.

He wadded up the paper and threw it at the messenger. The ruler of the dark elves' daughter was to be wed and to an above worlder elf. His right arm shot out, and he seized the messenger by the throat choking out any utterance from the frightened Illanni. The messenger knew that with only a little more effort, Tibersu's great strength could easily break his neck.

Instead, Tibersu drew the mortal forward and sank his fangs into the terrified underling's juggler vein. The fresh infusion of blood calmed his temper and eased the pains that had begun to build over the past turns of the clock.

After sating his hunger, he dropped the husk of the body to the ground. This one—this chattel, Tibersu thought—was now consumed and would not be given the power of new life as a vampire. Whoever dared bring him such news deserved this death.

The ruler of the Illanni paced the flagstone floor of the temple that had once been dedicated to their god, Taza. Tibersu's people had been lied to, and after their god had been destroyed in the Great War, Tibersu himself, in a fit of rage, had decapitated the statue of Taza by exploding its head with a lightning bolt.

The dark elf still felt betrayed. Taza's call to vampirism had merely been a ruse, albeit a worthy one, but it had consumed and destroyed many of his people. Afterwards, the remaining, but leaderless vampires had been sent scurrying back to the underworld city in panic, and they looked to him to rule Illan and guide them out of their time of crisis.

He had been more than ready to assume the mantle of ruler and if it meant ruling with an iron fist, so be it.

It was still the harsh role that Tibersu practiced.

•   •   •   •   •

After a long and tedious return trip to Illan, Martish and two of her most trusted soldiers now carried the chest into the temple. Their liege Tibersu was sitting at his table, and they placed it in front of him.

A monk came running up to the treasure, ready to open the crate, after her two soldiers had retreated from the room to stand guard at the door. They had never fought a vampire before, but Martish's orders had been firm. No one was to enter the room while she was alone with Tibersu.

A quick backhand from Martish sent the monk sliding several feet across the slick marble flooring.

Martish's voice was like gravel.

"I was instructed to deliver this to you alone, Lord Tibersu, not to any lackey.'

Tibersu laughed.

"There are too many distrustful fellows in Illan these days. Come let us open it and see the treasures that lie within."

He bent over the chest and broke the wax seals. With a deep breath, he opened the top. The treasures were all wrapped and seemed a little anticlimactic, but there was a wide smile on Tibersu's face.

First, he took out a long object, a sword rather simple in observance. Tibersu tossed it to Martish.

"Payment for a deed well done."

The sword felt light as a feather to her, but she would learn its true nature later.

Next Tibersu took out a bag and tossed it to Martish,

"Payment to your company."

The undead lord took several bags out and peered inside them and deposited them into his pockets. He pulled out another sword that he put aside for his own personal use. Finally, Tibersu took out a beautiful necklace with a blood red jewel set in its center. He quickly slipped it over his head and shut the case.

"Tell me, Martish, who held such treasures…and explain why they would be given over so freely."

She hesitated and then said, "A dragon, my lord. A giant dragon, black in color, and claiming to be have come through the void when the other dragons came to Muiria. I saw great wisdom in its eyes…and great cruelty. It said that the goddess Adois had promised it healing and treasure for these."

Tibersu nodded his head. He already knew that Adois had arranged this, but he had wondered what treasures she had given the dragon in exchange. He was curious about this black dragon and asked Martish to tell him everything else that she knew about him.

When she had finished, he dismissed her and pondered for a while. Adois was a schemer and a manipulator who hated and was jealous of her twin brother, Adaman…so much so that she would do anything to overthrow his power over Muiria.

With Taza dead, she had turned to him, Tibersu, to pick up the torch and carry on her fight to overcome this world. Somehow, he felt that the black dragon would play a part in that fight.

But what that part would, or when it would be played, was anyone's guess.

CHAPTER SEVEN

That, however, had also been Taza's dream...that and world domination. The Illanni leader vowed that he would succeed where his false god had failed. Time did not matter with Tibersu's efforts. He would wait and build up his forces until more and more could be released upon the world.

Since his last meeting with the Illanni's true vampire goddess, Adois, he had debated with himself about whether to ask her for more help. He did not want to incur her wrath, though, and he decided to wait and see what her gifts would do to help further their cause. With her aid, his people could more effectively direct their ire toward their distant kin.

Already his plans had been set into motion, but Tibersu still pondered his decision about whether or not to appeal to her sense of revenge. He hesitated still, but a sharp pang of fear shot through his veins.

If Tibersu hadn't been so angry with his false god, he might have felt sorry for him and the hell he must now be suffering for eternity.

Tibersu's earlier fit of rage had come from the message about his daughter, Morganna. She had escaped being turned into a vampire by using powerful magic, far beyond her age. Where she had gained such knowledge was still a mystery, but she had become one of the outlawed leaders of the underground movement trying to save the Illanni traitors unwilling to be turn into the vampires.

That his own daughter would go against his wishes was bad enough, but from the missive he had just read, Tibersu had learned that she was going to marry a Wood Elf.

Such an abomination was a shameful atrocity that could not be tolerated.

Striding over to the headless statue, Tibersu shouted up at it.

"Why did you make fools of us? Most would have gladly accepted your gift, but your drive to be worshiped all over the world has betrayed our clan."

He took one more quick step forward and used his vampiric strength to topple the remnants of the statue to the floor. He would have it removed later.

There would be no more foolery, no more back-stabbing, he decided. With or without Adois' help, it was time for the Illanni to step to the forefront and seize their rightful place on the planet.

CHAPTER SEVEN

Months later, Tibersu sat quietly at his desk. Four of his generals stood silently in plate mail armor, intently watching him. He turned to address them.

"Is she here?"

Martish stepped forward from the shadows.

"I am here, my lord."

Tibersu looked her over and noticed for the first time the change in her skin color after having adventured above the underworld. Had he been growing lax not recognizing the different color of her skin before this? Was she competent enough to trust? She wore a multilayer cloak and he saw the leather armor covering her arms and peeking through the front of the voluminous cloak.

"Can you get me to Ravannhiel?" he asked.

"I have come to know the forest well," she replied, not fazed by his question. "Using a powerful spell, you can easily enter the forest with the appearance of a forest elf."

Tibersu nodded.

"You will take a small company to Ravannhiel," he said. "I wish to attend my daughter's wedding. You are dismissed. The head priest will fill you in as to what your duties will be."

She bowed and backed out of her lord's sight. She trusted no one there and she drew her dagger as she sought out the head priest.

Lord Tibersu had let it slip that his daughter was getting married. Martish had heard the rumors that Morganna had fought against her people. And now marriage? It could only be to one of their enemies, possibly a wood elf.

It could hardly be, she thought, but she could not stop the tingle of delight knowing that it would cause her lord misery.

The light breeze did little to cool the lathered horses as their hooded riders drove them mercilessly toward the forest of Ravannhiel. It was as though the hounds of hell were nipping at their heels, but it would be dawn soon and the riders needed shelter and a place to rest.

Ahead, their scout awaited them atop a rise in the road his horse clearly winded. The twenty riders reined in as they reached him, and the scout pointed to a small farmhouse and barn.

To the west they could just make out the forest of Ravannhiel, shrouded by an early morning mist as the eastern sky grew lighter with the rising sun. The leader of the riders nodded and the others spurred their horses and joined the scout in a race for shelter.

Tibersu and his wife waited only a few clicks of the clock before uncaringly setting their spurs to their animal and with their steeds soon wheezing in great breaths of air, their sides bloodied, they steered the horses down the slope toward the others already at the farmhouse.

When they reached their destination, Tibersu and his wife dismounted. Their mounts were led to the barn to join the others' horses, which had no bloody sides.

Martish called out to one of her soldiers.

"Send the heeler to see to the wounds on their horses. We can't have them becoming infected and slowing us down."

The farmhouse consisted of two rooms, one for everyday chores and one for sleeping. The door to the farmhouse had been wrenched from its hinges by Martish's advance party, and the awakened family had been herded into a corner of the main living area.

Tibersu and his wife had not yet fed that day. Now that they had shelter; they eagerly approached the humans. Tibersu removed his hood, revealing the pale sharp features of an Illanni. He advanced on the family, his wife close behind. As they neared the terrified people, he drew back his lips and showed the humans the inch-long fangs of a vampire.

The family began to scream and Martish turned away as the two vampires slated their thirst. Martish had spread out her twenty soldiers around the house, but not one cared to stay in the cottage with the vampires.

Finally, Martish had had enough and she spoke up as they were about to take the child.

"My lord and lady, leaving the little one alive will further alarm the countryside to our presence and show them that no one is safe in all the land."

Lord Tibersu, fresh blood covering his face, looked at Martish.

"I think you are getting too soft, commander, but I see your reasoning. Tie the child up. We'll leave as soon as night falls."

Martish grabbed the crying child by the arm and led him outside to the barn and tied the child to a wooden post.

"Not a sound. Don't try to escape. I'll slit your ropes before we leave."

She stepped outside and called to one of her soldiers.

"Go to the barn and watch over that young human. Do not harm him in any way, or I'll have your heart."

•　　　•　　　•　　　•　　　•

The city of Menelwyn and the nearby forest of Ravannhiel were filled with elves, humans and dwarves, all coming together to celebrate a double wedding. Eldahir, son of Orthorion and one of the Wood Elves' greatest generals, was wedding Morganna, a former Illanni magically transformed into a wood elf. The other couple was Prince Tarquin of Parthia and his fiancée Ress, a commoner who had fought side by side with her husband to be and with others to defeat one of the world's greatest villains, Taza, the vampire warlock.

The royal wedding of a Parthian Prince—whose people were friends and allies to the elves—was looked upon as a joyous event, but the wedding of Eldahir and Morganna drew more than a few frowns and disgruntled remarks. The Wood Elves were a proud people and they would have been far more accepting if Morganna had been a High Elf or even a human.

Before the first battle at Zeiglon had torn the landscape of their continent asunder, all elves had belonged to a single nation. Now the changing landscape and the growing differences between them, however, had divided the once proud nation into three separate clans. The Wood Elves had remained in Ravannhiel, but the clan of High Elves had pushed east over the Mordolwyn mountains and settled in the Forest of Korvanna. The hardest hit by the devastation of the land had been the group now known as the Illanni. They had sought shelter underground and the hardship and deprivation they had suffered changed them from elves of light to dark elves.

The only reason the marriage of Eldahir and Morganna had been allowed to take place in the Wood Elves' homeland was that Queen Elornith had decreed it. Grateful for the part her faithful Lord Eldahir and Morganna had played in saving their homeland, the queen felt that it was the least she could do. Because so many Illanni had fled the vampires that overran their underground home, she also had felt it necessary to welcome them back to Ravannhiel.

She was even making plans to try and reunite the elves of light into a single united people once more, although negotiating this pact with the haughty high elves would be a monumental task.

The day of the wedding both brides looked breathtakingly beautiful. The elven queen had gifted Morganna with a bridal gown of the finest elven silk, bedecked with freshly plucked flowers of Edelweiss and daisies, and more of these flowers also adorned her veil and bouquet. Tarquin's parents, King Benton and Queen Alicia, had a gown made for Ress of white satin, decorated with seed pearls and Chantilly lace. A string of pearls had been woven through the long strands of her lush red hair and she carried a bouquet of white roses picked from the Queen's own garden.

The men also looked their best. Tarquin was dressed in the navy-blue finery of the Parthian royal family, and Eldahir wore his uniform of the Queen's Royal Troop.

Tarquin's best man was his dear friend, Botreg, a former dwarvan assassin and fellow Borderer, who fought beside him at the dwarvan stronghold of Brackus and Zeiglon. He also bravely fought at the battle of Dragon Isle. Tarquin's choice of best man had surprised his parents, who had thought that Tarquin would ask his only remaining brother, Prince Timmons…especially after the boys' eldest brother and heir to the throne, Prince Kaleb, had been killed in the war against Taza at the dwarvan stronghold of Southgard.

One other unusual turn of events was that the ceremony would be presided over by the dwarvan cleric Baldo another veteran of the wars.

CHAPTER EIGHT

At the wedding hundreds of guests looked on as the two couples said their vows and when the four sealed their unions with a kiss, a mighty cheer arose.

As they exited down the long aisle, all the families and guests rained white flower petals down on them like a gentle, celebratory snow fall.

Later, as the sun began its descent in the west and left faint beams of light to filter through the trees, the wedding party mingled about a wide, tented area. All the canopy sides were left open to catch the evening breeze and the guests dined on tasty fare that included roast lamb, venison, and pork, freshly picked vegetables, potatoes, sweetbreads, and a variety of desserts, including sugared fruits, hot pasties, and, of course, wedding cake.

The woods around the party were bedecked with flower garlands and lit by hanging lanterns that cast all the grounds in a merry glow. Dressed in their finest clothes, the guests were enjoying the reception and, fortunately, most of them were happy for Morganna. The only disappointed guest was the dwarvan monk Hority, who despised baths was exiled to a corner away from the party with his own table for one and closely watched over by Botreg.

As the partying continued, a commotion broke out at one end of the wedding grounds. Light skinned, platinum haired, black-eyed Illanni had appeared and they shoved wedding guests out of their way with their bows and notched arrows. A communal gasp rose from the crowd and the dwarves drew their weapons as elves and humans looked on the fray in dubious fashion.

The Illanni made no move to lower their weapons but stood, waiting, until Tibersu, leader of the Illanni and the father of one bride, stepped forward.

He smiled and made sure that his elongated teeth were visible before he spoke to the anxious crowd.

"My daughter is having a wedding and her mother and I were not invited? This is the worst breach of etiquette I could imagine. Nevertheless, fear not, my cousins. We mean no ill will this night. The bride's mother and I just want to make an appearance to wish our daughter well.

"Know this. My family is dead," Morganna said to the crowd in a loud, clear voice. "They died to me when they became vampires." She turned to face her parents. "I abhor what you have become and want nothing more to do with any of you."

"My lovely daughter, speak not in haste," Larahi, her mother, said. "Our people are stronger now and most readily accept the gifts that our former leader bestowed upon us."

"And those who don't," Kalsti, Morganna's maid of honor and a close friend shouted out, "are hunted down and forced to become the monstrosity you now call a 'gift.'"

"Hush, youngling," Tibersu said, menacingly. "You don't understand what goes on here. I have come to see my daughter as well as issue a warning. Any interference by the elves of light with my people will result in outright war,"

Tarquin, his sword Dragon Bolt now drawn, saw the haughty expression on the dark one's face, and he knew that they had not just come for the wedding or to give a mere warning. This was a show of force, just as their previous raids had shown. They were letting everyone know that they could and would venture forth from the underworld and travel where they wanted, and that all elves should be wary.

Celedant the wizard eased over between a group of guests until he had an unobstructed view of the dark ones. He knew these vampires could not be trusted. They were reaching out with a dove in one hand, but with a dagger in the other. He ever so slowly began lowering his staff.

Queen Elornith stood on her feet, tall and proud, and spoke to the Illanni.

"Go forth from here and leave this ceremony in peace."

Tibersu was standing near a High Elf guard.

"Oh, I will leave in peace," he said.

With a quick movement that only a vampire could accomplish, he drew his sword and sliced the High Elf's head from his shoulders.

"This is but a warning!" he shouted as he turned to go.

Screams of outrage filled the forest around the wedding party.

When Celedant saw the dark one begin to draw his sword, he brought forth a blaze of energy, which shot out from his staff, narrowly missing Tibersu but struck his wife Larahi instead. Her body exploded into dust just as the head of the High Elf hit the ground.

The dark ones' leader screamed a banshee wail of pain and defiance. "Noooo!"

The vampire's company quickly shot a wave of arrows into the wedding crowd, but several elvan soldiers quickly stepped in front of the queen and one took an arrow to the heart which killed him on the spot. Several other wedding guests were hit by the Illanni arrows, but their wounds were nothing that the assembled clergy could not treat.

Hority's table was close to where the dark ones had first interrupted the party. He raised his magical branch and ran toward the Illanni shouting, "Foes!" He reached them as they were leaving and he touched one with his branch. Its body fell forward, dead, and right onto Hority himself and entangled itself with the monk so much that he could not strike another dark one down.

The Illanni retreated into the gloom of the forest.

Several Illanni soldiers, including Martish, had to drag Tibersu away after he had kneeled next to the remains of his wife. If only she could leave him to be captured by the wood elves, Martish thought, but she had sworn an oath to him. She joined the others as they disappeared into the forest as silently as they had appeared.

General Orthorion ordered patrols and scouts to pursue the retreating Illanni.

The barrage of arrows had wounded several elves, and they were being attended to by healers. It would take a lot more than a single arrow to kill an elf…unless it was a perfect shot.

Martish and the others had dragged their lord from the wedding and as soon as they reached their horses, Martish dared to slap Tibersu on the cheek.

"If you don't gain control of your faculties," she said, "we will all die here. Come. Mount up now. They will have patrols out."

Tibersu held his hand to his cheek and was about to draw his sword when he thought better of it. The truth of Martish's words remained in his mind. Jerking the reins from his subordinate, he quickly mounted his horse.

The warlock standing nearby him cast a spell that made the company appear as wood elves, and they rode off making for the realm's border.

After several miles Martish's command crossed paths with a patrol of elves. Martish reined her horse in to keep from running into the enemy, but one of her soldiers was not as fast as she and collided with a wood elf. Their collision caused the warlock's spell to be lifted and suddenly the patrolling elves were staring at a company of dark elf Illanni horsemen.

Martish, the lead rider, whipped her sword out and gutted her opponent.

Soon the horsemen were entangled in a mass of swinging swords. The Illanni fared better than the wood elves had thought they might because these were Martish's personal raiders and they were used to fighting on horseback.

"Protect Tibersu," Martish shouted amid all the swirling blades.

At that moment a wood elf, his sword raised, rode up beside the vampire leader. Tibersu, trusting his vampire abilities, bore no sword, but an Illanni raider slammed his horse into the rear of the attacking wood elf and the rider was tossed over the head of the horse.

Martish was in the thick of things and fighting off two wood elves on either side of her horse. She parried both right and left and then both the elves attacked at the same time and she leaned backward and flattened herself the best she could as the blades passed within inches of her body. She felt the wind caused by the swords as they passed over her and then she was upright again fighting them off.

Suddenly an arrow appeared in the chest of one rider and thrust him off his horse. With one of her attackers now down, Martish turned her attention to the second and going on the offensive, she swung once overhead and beat the other's sword downwards. Suddenly she changed her sword's direction and stabbed the elf so deeply through his thigh that her blade passed through his saddle and entered into the horse. The elf's steed felt the sting of pain and leaped forward away from Martish.

Her sword was still stuck through the saddle, deep into the horse, and it was almost wrenched from her hand. Thanks to the leather strap around Martish's wrist and the strength of her arm, honed on the battlefields, she was able to pull the sword free.

As quick as it began, the fighting was over. The wood elves had withdrawn, followed by a lightning bolt from Martish's warlock.

Martish heard the blowing of battle horns, summoning more soldiers, and she ordered her company to see to the wounded and follow her. They rode fast through the forest, limbs beating against their bodies, and soon they were clear of the woods. Martish knew they had but six or seven turns of the clock to find a resting place for Tibersu.

Suddenly an enemy arrow struck one of her soldiers and she cursed her master. They needed to find shelter for him before the wood elves caught up to them. Quickly she led her command across the Ammiol river and out of the wood elves domain altogether.

Across the river the land was of made up of small, rising hills and the Illanni wasted no time in heading east toward the Mordolwyn mountains. As the sun was lighting up the eastern mountains with a glow along their peaks, Martish saw exactly what she wanted, an old dry river bed.

She pulled her horse up and shouted back to her troops.

"There! Stack the stones for Tibersu and give him several cloaks to conceal him from the sun."

She rode over next to the still grieving vampire.

"My lord, we must hide you and deal with any pursuers. The cloaks were designed to keep the sun out, but will cover you well. Then we wait until dark."

The vampire wasted no time and he slid off the horse and raced to his bedding. When he reached the small raised pit, he dove under the cloaks and several Illanni soldiers made sure the sun could not penetrate through the rock barriers they'd just constructed or the cloaks they'd put over their leader.

The company camped in the river bed that had formed many years ago before the water had dried up, but not before it had eroded the many hills once surrounding it. Morganna placed her soldiers in defensible positions around the riverbed. She knew that sooner than later the wood elves would come and she told her subordinates to release their horses, hoping they would lead the elves onwards even though she doubted that would happen. It was impossible to hide the tracks made by the horses in their escape.

If Tibersu were not with them, she knew they could have easily made it to safety, but now they were anchored to one spot with probably half the elven army still on their heels.

Soon enough a single rider reined up at the edge of the river bed and scanned the area before riding off back toward the west. The Illanni just waited, concealed in the tall grass or behind the small stunted trees. The scout had been barely thirty feet from one of Martish's soldiers.

Soon the Illanni heard the elven search party clomping up the riverbed and maneuvering across the rocky soil.

Martish had placed herself ten paces away from Tibersu and she waited and waited. The elves were taking their time and trying to follow the Illanni horse' tracks. Then they appeared. When the elves reached several paces from her, Martish stood and shot the first elf out of his saddle. Before the elf hit the ground, she had another arrow out and was releasing it.

She knew that the Illanni were now fighting all along the walls of the rock barriers and their arrows were pouring into the wood elves' ranks.

She also knew that eighteen bowmen and a lone warlock could not keep a hundred wood elves pinned down for long. Soon the riders were topping the walls and engaging the Illanni from horseback. Sabers rose and fell on top of the Illanni soldiers and they were eventually driven to the ground, some with grievous wounds. Martish had herself taken a backhanded saber blow to the head that had knocked her backward onto the rocky soil.

None of the Illanni had died, but the wood elves collected the unconscious ones and marched the uninjured down against a steep bank of the dry riverbed. The wood elves had also easily noticed the disturbed rocks and had quickly found where Tibersu was hidden.

The commander of the wood elves stood with his second in command beside the piled rocks and the two of them talked over what to do with the vampire. Should they remove the cloaks and let it disintegrate in the sun, they wondered together, or should they attempt to bring it back to their queen? Finally, the commander went over to the Illanni where Martish now stood unsteadily.

"You are the commander of this raid?" he asked her.

Martish nodded her head. She put her hands to her knees and began throwing up. The head wound had hurt her far more than she had realized, but once she had wiped her mouth with her arm, she answered their commander.

"I am Martish of the Illanni and I command here."

"You will all die for what you have done," the wood elf told her.

Martish heard the distinct sound of horse hooves, and all around the top of the river bed appeared the remainder of her company, sitting on their horses, bows drawn. They tossed down four round objects and with a thud four elven heads rolled to a stop amid the dismounted elves on the ground.

One of the Illanni on horseback called down to them.

"Your scouts, I believe."

The elven commander was appalled. Martish could see revenge and rage briefly pass over the elf's face, but she knew he would lose the battle if he charged the Illanni occupying the heights. Slowly the elven commander lowered his weapon and tossed it to the ground. His command followed suit.

Martish and the Illanni stood silently and waited for the sun to get low enough in the sky that only a soft red showed from the west. The wood elves gathered themselves together and stood silently as well. Finally, Martish went up to their leader.

"You are free to go back to your forest. Your horses will be released in time and I'm sure they will return home. I want you well away from here, though, before my master awakes and orders the death of your company."

The wood elf gave a curt nod, not deigning to speak to an Illanni.

"Let this be a warning to you that your borders are not safe, and that we will strike at any time," Martish told him,

She then proceeded to Tibersu's cairn to await the final disappearance of that day's sun.

CHAPTER NINE

The High Elves attending the dual wedding had gathered their fallen comrade's body, wrapped it in several cloaks and carried it away.

Queen Elornith then approached the leader of the High Elf delegation.

"This will not go unavenged," the leader of the delegation said to the Queen. "To bring death and vileness to such a joyous occasion is unconscionable."

"I assure you," the queen said, "we will not allow what has occurred this night to go unchallenged, and we offer whatever assistance you might need to avenge the death of your countryman."

"We would appreciate whatever aid you offer," the High Elf Ambassador said giving a slight nod to the queen. "I'm not sure how you see this, your highness, but I'm certain my own Queen and King will see it as an act of war."

"As do I," she replied solemnly.

•   •   •   •   •

Boltrein, Morganna's brother, was in the stables feeding on a cow's blood. He still refused the taste of any Illanni or the blood of another subject. Still, his forcible turning had aroused a sense of rebellion against his people's vampiric habits.

As he finished with the cow, he applied pressure to the vein and closed it before one of his guards found him.

"My lord, there is a messenger at the gate from your father," the guard announced.

Boltrein nodded, wiped the blood from his mouth with a handkerchief, and followed the guard out to the double-sided wrought iron gate. There awaited a lower level vampire, obviously still insulted by the guard's refusal to allow him in the estate. It had to be one of his father's newest followers, but his name escaped Boltrein.

"To what do I owe such a visit of one of my father's messengers?" Boltrein asked after acknowledging his presence by bowing his head to the visitor.

The barb struck home, and Boltrein could see the vampire grit his teeth. Control was the backbone of Illanni society, but here was one who had apparently digressed since his turning. Hence, he was now an errand boy.

The vampire drew himself up and bluntly stated, "A message from your father. You are wanted at the temple immediately."

"I will be along in a moment." Turning, Boltrein waved his hand and dismissed the messenger altogether.

What his father wanted was beyond his understanding. Now the black sheep of the noblest vampiric household, Boltrein was normally left alone.

Dressed in somber black, as was the fashion of the Illanni, he mounted the best horse from the stable. It was not far to the temple complex, but the son of Tibersu would be expected to ride rather than walk.

The populace had begun to travel in armed packs to scare off any would-be rogue vampires looking for blood, but Boltrein saw little traffic on the street today. Rarely did a single Illanni ever venture far from their house or estate.

He arrived at the courtyard of the temple of Adois, a many storied building made from quarried stone with a wide flight of stairs leading upward across the front of the temple. The temple had numerous balconies that stared like empty eye sockets over the city.

A cleric in a blood red habit hustled up to Boltrein to take his mount, and the Illanni leader's son climbed the great marble steps that led up to the temple proper. Before he reached the top of the stairs and the first level, he adjusted his clothes and made sure his sword was loose in its hilt. He could never trust his father's intentions, and he would not be caught unaware.

Boltrein was met by one of his father's minor clerics, who bowed to him and began leading the dark elf into the temple proper. He zigged and zagged his way through the meandering passages of the temple's first floor.

In several clicks of the clock, Boltrein was at the huge double doors that led to his father's chamber. He knocked and heard a muffled, "Enter."

The door was terribly heavy and only Boltrein's vampiric strength allowed him to easily open it with one hand. A normal Illanni, even using his whole-body weight, would barely crack open the doors.

Tibersu stood at a railing at the far side of the open room and was looking out over the courtyard.

"Do you like needling my messengers?" he asked his son.

Boltrein laughed.

"It was too easy. He was angry for having to wait. I just made him a bit more disturbed."

"Yes," his father replied. "He did complain, and I hate complainers."

He turned and tossed bag at Boltrein's feet. His son opened it and found that it was full of ashes. Boltrein examined it and then dropped the bag like it was of little importance.

Tibersu laughed.

"It is what is left of that messenger."

"Is it, kill the messenger, or don't kill the messenger?" Boltrein asked. "I tend to get the rules confused."

The unexpected humor caused his father to chuckle.

"I take liberties with sayings such as that." Tibersu said, but his smile disappeared before he continued. "I called you here to tell you that your mother was killed by the Wizard Celedant, and that your sister has taken one of the Wood Elves as a husband."

He cared little that his mother had died for she had been one of the Illanni who had held him while his father had turned him into a vampire. Since that day she had never spoken to him again.

Knowing that his spies had been right all along he had to tread lightly. Lying to his father was a dangerous endeavor. His sister was another thing. He felt inward revulsion that she would marry one of their hated cousins and at first, he hoped the information had to be incorrect.

"Father, Morganna would never take one of those abominations to be her husband."

Tibersu laughed cruelly.

"Your care for your sister is appalling, but your mother and I saw it transpire. It was at their wedding that your dear mother was killed by some sorcery. Do you not mourn for your mother's death?"

Boltrein shrugged.

"She was already dead to me, as you well know. She and I had not spoken since my turning. The care you apparently perceived was that of disgust at Morganna's unnatural union with a Wood Elf. I find it repulsive to even utter it out loud."

His father bowed.

"I did not mean to insinuate anything. I thought that you needed to know of the two events. You may go now, my son."

Being called son by Tibersu brought bile rising up the back of Boltrein's throat. He could not help but try to leave with the last word.

"I suppose that 'don't kill the messenger' applies to this situation?" he said to his father.

Tibersu laughed and waved his son away.

Boltrein had always known that power would corrupt, but he felt it had driven his father a bit mad as well. He quickly exited the building and took his horse from a habited cleric. Once mounted, he turned away from the dead-eyed temple and cantered out of the courtyard. He knew full well that his father was watching everything and he sat straight in the saddle and continued riding away from the temple at a slow pace.

Once he reached the streets of the surrounding city, the tall houses seemed to close in on him and made everything much darker. The hair on the back of his neck stood on end and he felt like he was being watched.

Without moving his head much, he scanned the area. With his keen hearing, he detected a barely audible scrape of leather on stone. Without warning, a dark shadow launched itself down from a third story window above Boltrein.

The Illanni vampire moved with a speed that only one of the turned could manage and he had his sword out before the falling figure struck. His feet already out of his stirrups Boltrein pivoted and dropped to the stone street while his attacker rolled once after he landed and got up in a crouch, his sword at the ready. With a snarl clearly marking him as a vampire, the Illanni assassin attacked.

Boltrein turned his attacker's sword aside and placed his own shoulder into the vampire's chest. The solid thump knocked him back a foot and then their swords danced. Back and forth across the road, the two fought, their swords like lightning, here, there, and gone in an instance.

Boltrein received a deep cut to his ribs but ignored the wound as only one of the undead could. He soon gave as good as he had gotten. In an instant both vampires had bleeding wounds about their bodies.

Boltrein wasn't a bad swordsman, but his opponent was far better and Boltrein was impressed with his attacker's skill and had serious doubts that he could win this fight. He retreated and tried to think of a way to defeat his foe.

Finally, Boltrein scissored his legs about his attacker. The assassin went down, but Boltrein was ready and as the Illanni hit the ground, Boltrein's sword was already in motion. It took his attacker precious clicks of the clock before he could react, and by that time Boltrein's sword had severed his opponent's forearm and had slashed halfway through his neck.

Boltrein jumped up as his attacker struggled to stand, but the vampire assassin could only drop his sword to grasp his neck. Boltrein finished him off with a quick backhand that severed his hand and then the rest of his head. His body burst into ashes.

As he collapsed to the ground, Boltrein heard himself gasping for breath and was surprised because he had thought a vampire would never do that since, in essence, he was already dead.

Boltrein found his horse down the alley, where it had run to for safety, and bruised and bloodied he remounted. Boltrein could feel the ache of the wounds, but that was inconsequential for a vampire. He rode hard for the estate, and his wounds already began to heal.

In his mind he replayed his meeting with his father and remembered the parting remarks. When Boltrein had quipped, "This is not the time to kill the messenger," his father had laughed, but had he known that Boltrein, his eccentric son, would soon be attacked on his ride home?

He did not put that beyond his fathers' capabilities.

Reaching the estate, Boltrein's guards took his horse and he retired to the house. The head servant approached him and waited for instructions.

"I believe these clothes are ruined," Boltrein said. "Please have a fresh set laid out for me."

Boltrein hated the fact that his sister had turned her back on her clan, but she had been treated so hard by their father and mother. She had escaped the curse they had inflicted upon him. It was no wonder she had then taken to the overworld, he thought, but to betray his love for her through this marriage to a wood elf was unacceptable. But, in the back of his mind a small tinkling of love for his sister came to the surface.

CHAPTER TEN

Tarquin and his friends joined the others at the Queen's table where King Benton, General Orthorion and Queen Elornith occupied the other chairs.

Hoity was sulking once again for being put at a separate table where Botreg the dwarvan assassin could keep account of him. The former Borderer was finding it hard to sit at the small table due to the ripe smell emanating from his tablemate and Botreg developed a new admiration for Baldo's perseverance at taking care of the filthy dwarf.

The cleric of Thierry had arrived to help his brothers in their transition to a new abbot and he had also vowed to rid the east of any enemies that had escaped there following the battle of Southgard.

Once all the company were seated, Queen Elornith spoke.

"What are we to do? My general's son has married an Illanni whose family came to the wedding and killed a soldier of the High Elven King and Queen...as well as one of my house guards."

General Orthorion spoke the words that the other elves had as yet only voiced in the shadows of that dark night.

"Son," he said to Eldahir, "you did not tell me that Morganna was Illanni and daughter to their ruler. Was this a deception on your part? To look at her, I would think her to be of Wood Elf in origin."

Eldahir cleared his throat.

"I did not tell you because I knew what your reaction would be. I—and many here—trust Morganna with our lives. She fought by our side during the war and saved more than one of our companions. It is true she was born favoring her ancestors, the Wood Elves. For this, she has always been persecuted by her father as well as other Illanni. In payment for the heroic deeds she has done and her decision to fight on the side of light over evil, the dwarvan god, Dolgar, finished the purification process. What you see is no deception. Morganna is now pure Wood Elf."

General Orthorion visually examined Morganna and then turned his gaze to his son.

"I believe you, son. Do your friends also vouch for her?"

"We do," Celedant, Azimuth and the others replied.

Azimuth added, "I give you my word as a dragon that Morganna's heart and mind are pure. Unlike her clan, she was somehow born without the darkness that infests those Illanni who welcomed the cloak of vampirism. Dolgar saw this, too, and that is why he intervened on her behalf."

Before the general could reply, a brilliant light shot into the room, and Dolgar stood before them in his immaculate, clean blue robes. The dwarves in the room, even Botreg the ex-assassin, knelt before one of their gods.

Dolgar spoke.

"As ye know, dragons do na lie. Nor do I. Rest assured that Morganna has no traces of dark elf within her. She is truly a creature of light. I meself have seen to her purification."

"If that is the case," Queen Elornith said, "Morganna is truly one of us. No one will deny her rightful heritage."

"I hope yer gods will lead ye in the right decision in these dark times," Dolgar continued. "Baldo, yer brethren need ye at the monastery. They need a steady hand to take over as their abbot. Botreg, me wayward son, please take care of poor Hority. His dedication to Clor is admirable, but it sometimes gets him into trouble."

With a flash of light, the dwarvan god disappeared.

Hority, who had been kneeling away from the table, prostrated himself on the ground, raised his face to the others and yelled loudly and passionately.

"We are in Clor's favor! Nothing can stop us in this venture!"

Botreg jerked him up by his armpits, forcefully placed him back in his chair and tried to calm down the agitated dwarf. If not for Botreg the dedicated monk would have rushed off to war against the dark elves alone.

"There is much to be collected and cataloged in the coming months," Botreg told him. "But please stay here and make not a sound." Answered Botreg.

The Clorian monk started jumping up and down again and held up his hand.

Celedant now motioned to him and Botreg was again up from the table and corralling the overly enthusiastic, musty smelling dwarf.

"I will stay silent. I promise," the dwarf finally said.

"If we may continue..." Queen Elornith said, her fingers tap-tapping on the table.

"I must ask you, Morganna," General Orthorion said. "Celedant killed your mother. Does that not distress you?"

"I don't wish to sound cold-hearted, but you must understand, sir. My parents forced my brother to turn and tried to do the same to me. The vampires are a scourge on my people. Many Illanni have fled their homes to escape a fate they consider worse than death. Our underground movement is constantly working to help others flee the capital Illan. I have vowed to help them in every way I can and hope that Ravannhiel will accept those returning to life above ground and welcome them into your community. I cannot change my heritage. I fought to escape the hell that Illan has become. My intentions are pure, to save my people and end the tyranny that grips Illan."

The others who had accompanied her on the quest for the staffs all gave vigorous nods of support.

Suddenly there was a great rustling of leaves from outside the chamber and something quite large alighted on the ground. Through the large window everyone saw a strikingly beautiful High Elf dismount from a dragon. As soon as she had moved several paces away, her dragon transformed into a female High Elf and together they entered through an open portal and approached the table.

"I am Gilraen Sindanarie, Princess and daughter of the High Elf King and Queen. As you know, my father and mother left a fortnight ago to see to the security of our homeland. I have come as an emissary of my people to add our voice to whatever plans must be made concerning this debacle."

Queen Elornith bowed her head.

"It is an honor to have a princess of the High Elves present."

The others rose from their seats in respect and Celedant, too, nodded to her. He was glad to have the High Elves join in these talks. She returned his nod with a smile and her female dragon, Silmarwen, greeted Azimuth, leader of all dragonkind, through her skills with telepathy.

"Do the Wood Elves make it a common practice to marry their fallen kin?" the princess asked. In response to their startled expressions, she added, "We have heard the rumors...even in Korvanna and many question the choice."

Her aloofness startled all but Celedant and he quickly spoke before the meeting turned ugly.

"Sorceress, our council deems that Morganna is worthy of our trust and has our needs foremost in her thoughts."

"I will withhold judgment until I see for myself," the princess said. "My King and Queen demand justice for what has happened under your roof. Also, several months ago a patrol of our most experienced soldiers were ambushed by these Illanni and slaughtered, leaving only the commander alive to bring the news to us. We pledge aid and soldiers to combat this plague."

General Orthorion glared at the pretentious High Elf.

"We are deciding that now. Such an incursion and foul murder cannot be abided."

"What do Celedant and Prince Tarquin have to say?" Queen Elornith asked.

"I'm tired of these vampires dogging my footsteps," Tarquin quickly replied. "Sending Taza to his demon goddess was only the first step. We need to strike at the heart of the matter."

"My young friend has an impertinent streak, but speaks the truth," Celedant added. "We thought we had ended the vampire problem with the death of their false god, Taza. The monsters are usually solitary creatures, yet the Illanni vampires appear to break that mold. It can be deduced that Lord Tibersu now holds sway over the Illanni. Break his hold on them, and this monstrous movement might just fall apart."

"Do you propose to destroy this abomination?" The high elf asked.

"There is no other way," Morganna interjected. "It is obvious that Tibersu plans to take up where Taza left off."

"As long as he and others like him live, they pose a threat to our two peoples," the general agreed. "He has shown us that he is willing to venture above ground and kill. If we wait, I am afraid these attacks will continue."

"Killing isn't what he has in mind," Morganna said. "He plans to turn as many denizens of Muiria as possible until the vampire scourge is so great that it takes over all the land like a plague."

"I agree," Azimuth leader of all dragon kind added. "And although this appears to be shaping up into a war between the Elvan clans, I pledge myself and my dragons to your aid."

"We can no longer consider the Illanni a lost people," the Queen said. "Mayhap our ancestors should have kept in contact with them. Then this might not have happened. But he holds our two clans responsible for the suffering his people have endured, and he means to exact revenge. It might be slow in arriving, but more Elven blood will be shed over this issue."

The general straightened up and said, "I will lead our best soldiers into the underworld and rid us of this pest."

Celedant offered his own gentle proposition.

"You are very brave my friend, and I believe you are right. Eventually we may have to face the wolf in his den. But we may spare countless lives if the battle remains above ground for as long as possible. In the meantime, I propose that I and several of my companions seek out Tibersu in his lair and end this threat. If the vampires become leaderless, it should throw them into chaos, if only briefly. That is when we strike to eliminate the rest of them."

"I was born in Illan," Morganna said, "and can lead a group through the warrens and into the city. I also have contacts with the underground that may prove useful,"

"For now, at least, I think you should concentrate your efforts on helping the Illanni who want nothing more than to escape the vampire's scourge," Celedant said. "They will be the initial targets. It will help our cause even more if we can prevent as many as possible from being turned."

"So be it," the queen said. "I agree with some of what Celedant says, but I too cannot allow what has happened to go unavenged." With steel in her voice she then commanded, "General, assemble as large a force as you deem necessary to assault the Illanni. I believe a show of force cannot be crossed out, considering where their attack took place, and we owe it to the High Elves to atone for the death of one of their own. We also need to reinforce both Ravannhiel and Korvanna to prevent raids against our people. Morganna, you prepare to infiltrate your old city."

Celedant silently cursed Tibersu before he spoke.

"The dark one has gotten what he wanted, a full-scale war…on his terms. General Orthorion may be pleased to take the battle to the dark ones, but a war in the netherworld would be difficult at best. Too many elves will die in the coming months."

However, the council endorsed war and there was no way he could advise against this. If only they had gone with his plan to cut off the head of the snake before going to battle…

The High Elf Princess added, "When the time comes, the King and Queen of Korvanna will lend aid to this endeavor by sending forces to assault the Illanni city. In the meantime, we will prepare our people for war and protect our borders."

"I would also like to enter into negotiations with your parents," Queen Elornith said. "If we are to welcome our fallen kin back to the surface, they will need a home to return to. I think it is time we discussed rejoining our clans into one Elven nation."

Gilraen, the High Elf, made a slight downward turn of one side of her mouth.

"The Illanni threat is of most import at the present," she said and then turned to speak privately with her dragon, ignoring the others there.

CHAPTER ELEVEN

Several weeks later Tibersu was still raging that his wife had been obliterated and he felt that that thoroughly proved the little trust he could put into the Wood Elves. Now the High Elves were involved, too, but that he could understand. After all, he had killed one of them and destroyed one of their patrols. Where could he turn now for counsel in this uncertain time, he wondered.

He had been pacing and when he looked up, Tibersu found that he had stopped in front of a statue of Adois, Taza's patron goddess. He knelt down before it.

All his long life he had believed in his own hand and not in any faith that would provide gains in this would. He was a vampire and he had settled down for a long wait. Now he did not know what exactly to do.

In his head he prayed, "Adois, I am in need of aid. I have taken up Taza's cause."

He knelt for almost a full turn of the clock until, suddenly, he heard a voice in his head.

"Dear Tibersu, open your eyes, please."

The dark elf opened his eyes and he was in an elegant chamber lit by a hundred candles. Reclining on a sofa in front of him was the beautiful Illanni woman, Adois. She motioned him forward.

"I welcome you, Tibersu master, of the Illanni. How might I be of service to you at this time?"

Tibersu drew himself up.

"I am at a crossroads and I know not which way to follow."

She chuckled.

"Men in need always seem to call on me. Why should I help one as powerful as the vampire ruler of the Illanni? I have already sent you aid in Taza, the one who started you towards the ultimate power of vampirism. What of the treasure of the dragon? What is it you want now?"

"I follow Taza's doctrines," he replied. "I want to see my people better themselves on the planet of Muiria."

At that she laughed.

"You dare preach to me about bettering your people? You, a vampire?"

"No, my lady," he floundered. "I only seek guidance, for I will soon make war upon the elves."

She held up her hand.

"Stop! I have heard enough. What doth thou have to give me?"

"I have only the devotion of my people and their willingness to become vampires...so we can save ourselves."

She waved away disdainfully any further groveling by the vampire.

"So, I repeat, what doth you need at this time?"

The Illanni stood tall.

"When we go to war, we would carry your banner before us, thus angering Adaman."

She leaned forward.

"Now that is an interesting proposal. I have failed with that useless Taza. Could you be my next? Hmm."

Tibersu spoke immediately.

"I could aid you, my lady. I could."

"Begging does not suit you, Lord Tibersu." she said. "I have an eternity to wait for my plans to reach maturation and you as an elf before, and now as a vampire, have many eons to work out my plans. Taza could not resist the need for time. He acted impatiently. Though a vampire, he had studied the humans to such an extent that he viewed the world the way that a short-lived race would. You, on the other hand, view the world through the eyes of an elf, a race to which time matters very little."

She seemed to Tibersu to be thinking for a moment. Then, with a flick of her hand she threw something at him. He caught it and found he was holding a small ring.

"That should protect you over the years," she said, "if you are careful and obedient. It can also be influential over lesser minds. Remember, nothing can make you invincible. That was Taza's major flaw. You would be wise not to forget that advice."

Tibersu felt lightheaded.

He found himself again lying on the floor in front of the idol of Adois.

"A mere ring, he shouted out. "What am I supposed to do with it?"

But there was no answering voice.

"Damn her," he yelled. "The gods and their banalities! What am I to do with this trifling gift?"

●   ●   ●   ●   ●

Morganna and Eldahir, their hands interwoven, made their way down the steep stairs to the forest floor where Baldo stood waiting for them. He had been their companion for many months, all the while in constant danger and he was now set to leave for the Theirrian Monastery this day. Tarquin and Ress had already been bidding the dwarf goodbye.

The dwarf was needed in the east to help clear the countryside of dangers and to help govern the monastery of Thierry since the abbot had died on the quest to reassemble the Staff of Adaman. The dwarves who had died during that quest were commemorated in a newly commissioned wall carving that depicted all the members of the quest and named them individually. Even the odd Clorian monk, Hority, had been added humorously, but standing several paces from the group. Tarquin and Botreg had been let go then from the Dwarvan King's Borderers in quite a ceremonial fashion due to their accomplishments.

Morganna and Eldahir stepped gently onto the forest floor and approached the gathered companions. Morganna stooped to Baldo and kissed him on both cheeks. She had learned that was a tradition of that race.

"It has been a pleasure to gain such a friend as you," the former Illanni said to him. "The dangers that we shared together have truly made you seem a part of my family, and I am sure my dear husband will echo my words. You are always welcome at our door."

"I wish our adventures were not to end now," Baldo said. "But needs at home call for me duty."

In a hushed voice he added, "Thierry sends word not to give up on your brother."

Hority, somehow quite clean today compared to his normal appearance, said, "I plan to stay a while longer."

Several of the elves wrinkled their noses, but a worried look crossed Hority's face.

"I just hope the Theirrians have not cleaned our valley too much," he said. He knew the former Abbot of Theirry had left a contingent of clerics to help the defenseless Clorians and to comb through their archives.

Botreg cuffed him playfully on the head, but only a small dust cloud rose from his hair today.

"Hority, I fear a hundred good monks of Theirry couldna change yer Clorians."

There was general laughter at the expense of the normally filthy dwarf.

"Come, Baldo, ye must leave before the sun is too high in the sky," Botreg added.

"My life is intertwined with yers Tarquin," Botreg said, "and thus I will stand by yer side."

Hority, not to be outdone, added, "Clor has sent me on a mighty quest to fight evil and I too am bound to ye, Tarquin, and to vengeance for our fallen friends."

Botreg now had to calm the dwarf down again, but Hority yelled, "Foes!" and ran off to war against the Illanni on his own.

Queen Elornith called after the departing dwarf.

"Baldo, the Mordolwyn mountains are crawling with orcs. Allow me to send a company of elves to offer you some protection. It is the smallest of things that I could do for a hero like yourself."

Baldo mounted his small mountain horse and with a wave goodbye, he set off down the elven trail followed by a company of elven guards.

The two newly married couples stood until Baldo and the elves disappeared from view behind the immense trees of Ravannhiel.

"Come," Ress said. "As our friend leaves us, we now have lives to share amongst our newly made families."

Celedant and Azimuth stepped out from the forest shadows. They had said their goodbyes earlier to Baldo,

"While we break our fast," Celedant said, "we must speak of the coming venture."

They all made their way back through the forest to a private room in the queen's palace. A table had been set with morning fare and as they broke their fast, there was silence while they gloried in the tasteful elven fare. Hority having been caught by the elves before he could get too lost in the forest was pouting. There was some grumbling, because he had been placed at a small table set aside from the others while Botreg oversaw his activities. No matter how many times he bathed, his habits remained intolerable.

Finally, Celedant asked the question that was on each of their minds.

"Now…what do we do?"

Ress spoke first. "It would seem that Morganna should tell us."

The transformed Illanni cleared her throat.

"There must be an entrance into the underworld nearby since Tibersu was able to make his way to our marriage. We must find it and enter that dark place I once called home."

"I will be able to find it with the help of the wood elves," Azimuth said. "I shall change into a wolf," the third form which a dragon could morph into, "and follow their scent back to the hole from whence they crawled."

"As will I my friend," interrupted a high elf who had just entered the room.

Celedant immediately chimed in.

"It will be a pleasure to have another sorceress accompany us on this mission. This is Inwe Culnamith. She was sent by the High Elven King and Queen to assist in our quest. She just arrived last night. Come now, Morganna, tell us what we must do."

Azimuth immediately rose and made his way over to another dragon who had appeared as a High Elf. He turned to the others and introduced him.

"Durring is from the distant Dragon Isle…"

The High Elf interrupted Azimuth and asked haughtily, "Are we to trust an Illanni renegade?"

Celedant instantly came to Morganna's defense before any of the others could voice an opinion.

"I trust her with my life," he said, "and I state that myself, as a wizard of Dragon Isle."

The High Elf acquiesced.

"That is high praise and I ask your pardon if I offered insult. We have been taught that the Illanni are not to be trusted and I am sorry for that misconception."

Morganna, the former dark elf now changed into a full wood elf, just bowed her head. She knew of the many years of a tradition of hatred that spanned the gulf between her race and that of the other elves.

"Kalsti and I know the underworld better than any," Morganna said. "If Azimuth can find the entrance, then we can lead a small party through its dangers and reach the city of Illan."

"Is there any way for the army to march through the tunnels of the underworld?" the queen asked.

"There are many wide passages there," Kalsti said, "and if we find the same one used by the Illanni, we will find that it is a large passage. After all, they led their horses through that dark place. But if I may be so bold, please let us first try to confront Tibersu. A war in the underworld is nothing to be desired."

For the first time General Orthorion spoke up.

"Evil deeds have been done to both our peoples," he said and nodded toward the High Elf. "We will strike at the heart of the evil and scour the planet of their transgressions into vampirism."

The queen clapped her hands together.

"So be it," she said, "that Celedant will go his way and we shall march on the city. May one of us, at least, be successful."

Morganna silently offered a prayer to the dwarvan god Dolgar that her brother Boltrein had not changed for the worst. That she could reach him in time to persuade him to help their cause.

CHAPTER TWELVE

Azimuth, Durring and the wood elves took longer than expected to find the hole from which the Illanni had issued forth like worms. Once it was discovered, a company of elves were left to keep watch for any activity. Azimuth transmuted into his dragon form and flew back to Menelwyn to meet in private with Queen Elornith, Celedant, Tarquin and general Orthorion.

He began by bowing to the queen and then reporting to all four.

"The cave that the Illanni exited is a week's ride from here. It is well hidden by trees and underbrush. Luck played a big part of our finding it at all, but we also discovered there a young human whose parents had been attacked by vampires. Interestingly enough, one of the Illanni had cut him loose and told him to hide until they had gone."

Orthorion spoke up, a growl in his voice.

"We will await the high elves and then march on Illan."

A messenger was dispatched to the high elves with the new information from Azimuth, and the high elves replied with a message of their own. They were mustering and would soon follow Inwe and Durring to Ravannhiel.

The high elves arrived the following fortnight. The wood elves were busy awaiting the time for their departure, to say the least, while their army began preparing the large supply of provisions and equipment they would need. According to Morganna and Kalsti the elvan soldiers would have to carry their provisions on mules and march on foot. That was the best way to move across the terrain of the underworld.

Their companions were also equipping themselves for their journey into the underworld and even Hority, much to his resistance, took a cleansing bath. Afterward the water was murky with the mud he had procured and he declared to Botreg that the mud had been white, so surely that was a sign of good things to come.

•   •   •   •   •

Celedant met in secret with General Orthorion concerning the upcoming mission.

"I disagree with the course this is taking..." the wizard began.

The wood elf general cut him off.

"I know of your warnings. I can read the concern in your eyes, but the die is cast and we will advance on Illan even though the high elves in their arrogance sent only a token number of warriors and magic users. Damn them all to the nine levels of hell."

"You cannot blame the arrogance of the high elves," Celedant said. "They are overly protective of their lands and just don't comprehend what is about to happen in the outside world. They believe elven arms will overcome their enemies.". Celedant mastered his composure and added one last objection. "You don't know the underworld and how dangerous it is. I have ventured there many times and have barely come out alive on numerous occasions. It is not just the Illanni. Many powerful monsters call the under-dark their home. You will lose many elves before you reach Illan. Let us go ahead of you and we will have a better chance at reaching Illan than all the elves you can summon.

The general shook his head.

"No, old friend. We must enter the caves or look weak in front of the high elves...and especially in front of the evil Illanni. If ever the princess's plan of uniting the clans is to come to fruition, we must cooperate in this venture."

Celedant looked defeated.

"Well, at least I hope to enjoy a glass of wine with you after this is over," he said.

•   •   •   •   •

When it was time to depart, there was much fanfare as elves lined the avenues waving flags and wishing their loved ones a safe journey. They tossed flowers and bouquets along the roadway and many of the soldiers picked them up and placed them in their sashes. The elven army had not marched out to war since the battle for Southgard, and many had not returned from that. Such a loss of their people had been hard for them to bare.

Elves believed they were meant to live an eternity, but they had lost their fellow compatriots in that battle and there had been many families mourning the loss of a loved one from that conflict.

Queen Elornith stood atop the gate house and wished the entire army good luck as they crossed beneath here, but tears started flowing freely down her face when she realized how many were marching away, perhaps to their death.

Her companions were standing alongside her, and Morganna, seeing the queen's tears, placed an arm around her and whispered in her ear before leaving her side to join the first ranks of the troops.

"What did you tell her?" Azimuth asked Morganna as she joined his side.

"I assured her we would get to Tibersu as quickly as possible and save the many lives that could otherwise be lost."

After a week marching night and day through the foothills and then into the Mordolwyn mountains they finally reached the entrance to the underworld. The company's humans and dwarves were hard put to keep up with such a constant pace, even on horseback, and they soon fell well behind. The elves then gave them magical herbs and wine that kept them riding onwards with the same endurance as the elves.

Finally, they reached the tunnel near a small depression in the ground that the elves, with the help of Azimuth and Durring, in wolf form, had detected and that marked the cave that the dark ones had used.

That night the army camped near the entrance and made sure everything, even the smallest item, had been packed for their imminent venture.

The Illanni resistance members were the first to enter into the tunnel that led underground and they spread out to follow the tracks that Tibersu's expedition had left. After going several miles, the tunnel branched out into three separate routes and the Illanni consulted the wood and high elves. The wood elf General Orthorion and the high elf General Rathar consulted one another and they agreed to follow the freed Illanni scouts.

"I am dubious of following any rebel, but in this situation, I deem it necessary," Rathar said.

Orthorion agreed. "Several rebel Illanni know of this intersection and advise taking the middle passage, the only one that could accommodate an army. Even

Morganna has vouched for its use. Besides, Tibersu's trail had gone cold once the tunnel became the bed rock of the mountain."

•   •   •   •   •

Once the head of the army began passing by Morganna and Kalsti into the middle tunnel, the two of them got into a heated debate concerning the passages and about which one to take. While they argued, the elven army marched silently past them.

"What seems to be the problem here?" Tarquin asked them.

Morganna looked at the human and explained their disagreement.

"We are in a quandary as to which passage to take. We can continue forward with the army and waiting for an attack as we slip away into passages now filled with Illanni, or we can take the right hand passage. It is a shorter distance to Illan, but much more dangerous. There are other evil things in the under-dark besides dark elves. To reach Illan this way is faster," Morganna insisted and pointed to the far right passage.

"There is a reason we do not use that tunnel," Kalsti argued. "It threads its way too close to our enemies, enemies that we have fought to a standstill. Many Illanni lost their lives trying to clear these tunnels."

"Does this tunnel really get too close to these enemies?" Tarquin asked Morganna.

"No," Morganna answered, "but it is close to their strongholds and those are sure to be patrolled."

Celedant came over to them and interrupted.

"A small group might be able to get past these dangers. This is much like the chance we had to take to recapture the dwarven city of Brackus."

Morganna reluctantly agreed.

"So, we take the southern passage," she said.

They bid the generals safe journeys and the wizard cast a spell on himself and Ress so the darkness of the tunnels would not be a problem. When the spell was cast on Ress she opened her eyes to find that she could see in the darkness. Tarquin had gained the ability fighting in the Dwarvan King's Borderers in the depths of the mountains. While the elves and dragons had no problems with such matters.

Boltrein was sitting in his father's study when there was a discreet knock on his door. He looked up from the papers he was reading and said, "Come in."

A thin dark elf slipped through the door his eyes scanning the whole room looking for enemies or traps.

"You need not worry. I am alone and you are always safe in my home. Also, what have you learned?" Boltrein announced.

The Illanni spoke in a whisper, "An elvan army has entered the under-world. It consists of both wood and high elves. Your sister is with them too."

Boltrein pondered this for a second and waved the spy away. He grated his teeth for a while a deeply hidden admiration arose concerning his sister. He wished her a safe journey. But, why? She had rebelled against the vampires sapping their strength by leading the rebel cause to get as many dark elves out of the city as could escape. She and her cohorts were weakening the Illanni clans and that could not be tolerated. Perhaps she could be reasoned with but if not she might have to be killed.

• • • • •

Deep in the caverns Celedant pointed at the ceiling.

"We must be careful," he said. "The roof of the cave seems unstable."

The natural passage contained many boulders that had dislodged from the roof of the cave since its creation and it took more time than they had for the company to wind their way through them without making any loud sounds that might echo down the tunnel. They were already having trouble enough with their gear making noises. Celedant whispered to Tarquin, "If Morganna is right enemies swarm through this cave system and the company needs to be extra quiet."

CHAPTER THIRTEEN

The Illanni rebels leading the army through the passages looked the part. They were all dressed in scavenged armor and had a myriad of weapons. They took several wood elves and high elves with them out in front of the army to scout the passages. The Illanni wanted to impress upon the elves that they were seen as trustworthy by having them join the Illanni scouts. The passage ran straight but had smaller corridors intersecting it at different points along the way.

After a full turn of the clock the advance soldiers spotted fire light in the distance and the elven scouts went forward while one of them returned to report to the generals.

"There is a troop of orcs camped directly ahead at the intersection of several passages," the scout informed the general. "From the smell they have been there for some time and must be guarding the passages for the dark Illanni."

General Orthorion grimaced.

"I had hoped to get along further in the tunnels, but we were bound to be found out sooner or later."

He turned to captains Arantir and Trimimar.

"Go. Take a company ahead and deal with the orcs. Try not to let any escape...but I fear that is a forlorn hope."

Three quarters of a turn of the clock had passed when the uproar started at the front of the elven column as the company of elves clashed with the orcs. The orc guards that had been posted up the passage from the elves were dispatched with elvish precision, their foot falls so quiet that the guards never heard or saw the wood elves. They slipped up behind the guards, clamped their hands over their mouths and neatly sliced each of the orc's throats.

The company of elves now gathered farther ahead at the mouth of the passage. Elven bows were drawn and their arrows shot silently out at the unsuspecting orcs in front of them. Many fell, and the elves drew their bows again. The second volley of arrows whistled by the attacking elves and killed another rank of the orcs.

One group of elves rushed forward, led by their captains, their weapons drawn. The elves had caught most of the orcs still in their bed skins and they barely had the time to draw their weapons before they were run through by the elves. Soon the elves and their enemies were locked in combat, but the superior training and better crafted weapons of the elven soldiers pressed the orcs backwards towards several tunnels. The wood elves swept through the huddled orcs and one by one killed their hated enemy as they advanced.

The wood elf Captain Trimimar was sickened, yet he ran his sword through a defenseless orc still tangled in its blankets. A last thought passed through his mind before crashing into the main fighting. "That orc probably had a family too."

One troop of elves was trying to get to the tunnels behind the orcs, but already many of their enemy were seeking to escape down them. The orcan leader had gathered enough orcs to make a stand and, with their shields interlocked, they now guarded their compatriots' escape path.

The elves crashed into the shield wall with an echoing clatter of swords. Arantir, not used to fighting on foot, paused a second as he searched for a place to attack. It looked to him like his command was just pushing the orcs backwards towards the tunnels. A spear thrown by one orc came shooting towards him, but he simply stepped aside and heard the impact of the spear on the elf following closely behind him. Looking back with concern at the soldier, Arantir saw that the spear had hardly pieced the elf's mythril armor. The elf just staggered backwards and a comrade dragged him from the fight.

The hand to hand combat continued to be deadly and neither side was giving an inch. Swords and a myriad of other weapons were swung with deadly force during the encounter and elves fell back, wounded, while orcs fell dead or escaped with their own wounds down the passage.

Soon the combination of elven weapons and arrows broke the orcs' courage and the rest fled down the passage, too. The elvan bowmen shot arrow after arrow at the furthest cave openings and brought down many orcs, but the will had gone out of their enemies and they all broke and ran.

The elves started to pursue them down the tunnels, but their commanders called them back before they had gone too far. The elven attack had been successful in destroying most of the orcs, but to many were still carrying word of the incursion back to their leaders.

The elves had only lost several soldiers and had a small number wounded that the clerics were quick to take care of. The dead elves were buried under cairns of stone and their bodies would be recovered when the army returned to the surface.

•   •   •   •   •

Cyra, the black sorceress of the west, was sure that her white orcs mercenaries would have reached the elven forest by now. They had been given the mission to camp outside of the towering trees of Ravannhiel and wait and the kill their prey. Cyra had not underestimated her foes and had sent over a hundred orcs that could lay in wait for the perfect time to attack and she had equipped them with a magic sphere that could direct them to the humans and their traveling companions. She had even used a crystal ball of her own making beforehand to identify and imprint the pictures of the company in the device.

She was hidden in a small house in the city of Trudoc when she activated the globe to communicate with her party of orcs. Once the leader came into to view, Cyra saw the concern on his face.

Across the miles she immediately asked, "What is wrong?"

Her commander grimaced once before answering.

"My lady, the situation has changed, but we have located the humans and other ilk that travel with them."

Cyra tried to keep her temper in check and said, "And…?"

The orc cleared his throat and began.

"Once we arrived, two giant wolves issued forth from the forest and several hundred elves followed them. Some time passed and two great dragons retired to the forest. Then an army of elves, thousands strong, marched forth. The sphere indicated our prey was traveling with that army."

Cyra looked hard at her minion. "Then what?"

He answered as calmly as he could.

"We followed in the steps of the army. They marched for a week, until they reached a cave. They entered and have not come out again. The elves have left a sizable company to guard the mouth of the cave with many more soldiers than in my company."

Across the many miles the sorceress could tell her captain was telling the truth. She thought for a while and came to a decision.

"Stay where you are and observe," she commanded. "The underworld might do your job for you. Wait and inform me immediately when they exit."

The white orc bowed his head and looked her in the eyes.

"I will do as you wish."

CHAPTER FOURTEEN

Morganna and Kalsti led the company downwards through the rock-strewn passage at a slow pace. While they were struggling through the passage, the company at one point came to a carved stair that led off to their right.

"This will take us even lower," Morganna whispered. "No one knows who delved these stairs. It may have been the Deprahs, and their warrens may be near."

Botreg and Hority both perked up.

"They are a mere fable. They do na exist," the dark dwarf said.

Celedant spoke up. "I too have heard of these Deprahs. I too have doubted they lived and have suspected they were just a myth."

"These animals are supposed to have been a clan of dwarves," Botreg said, "that journeyed south seeking shorter routes through the mountains. They corresponded with us for a year. Then nothing was ever heard from them. We sent a company of dwarves after them, but they lost their trail in the myriad of tunnels. It is said they are magical and can burrow straight through the stone...without any tools."

"We go on and deal with these creatures when and if we encounter them," Tarquin said. He had decided the matter.

Morganna led them down through a carved entrance way and into a corridor that turned left, and they began a fast walk down the smoothly chiseled passage. They had to spend several ticks of the clock in the passage until it opened out into a large chamber. It was there that Celedant and Inwe whispered "Hold!" at the same instance.

"I feel evil in this chamber," the wizard said. "Move cautiously."

They began crossing the room when out of the corner of her eye Morganna caught the flash of a spell being cast. She threw herself backwards into Ress as a jagged arc of lighting shot across the spot where she had been standing. It caromed off the rock wall and started back the way it had come before it finally sizzled out.

In the return of the darkness, dark Illanni soldiers attacked.

Ress and Morganna took cover. Meanwhile Eldahir and Tarquin sent their arrows flying in the direction of the spell caster while Botreg continued to arch his arrows at the enemy across the huge stone room.

Hority escaped the grasping hands of his friends and gave his familiar war cry, "Foes!" Then he was off into the darkness, swinging his branch this way and that, killing the Illanni with just a bare touch.

A darkened figure dropped down on to Inwe, but with ease she used her staff to first dislodge the attacker and then to cave in its head.

Meanwhile arrows shot back at them from all directions and one bounced off Tarquin's mail shirt. On the other side of the dark passage the Illanni spell caster stood to cast another arc of lightning.

Celedant had been biding his time for just that moment. He cast a quick and simple spell that sent balls of energy out at the attacker one after the other, the balls struck the dark figure and knocked it to the floor.

The others now rushed at their attackers and Tarquin hurried forward and tackled one enemy soldier just before it could discharge its bow. Tarquin saw that he was facing an Illanni dressed in dark black clothes who quickly recovered and drew a short sword. Tarquin, with the advantage, ducked under the wild swing and plunged his own sword into his attacker's chest.

All about the room the others were locked in mortal combat.

Ress was thrown down, but she plied her spear to good effect and lanced one of her attackers, pinning the Illanni to the wall before she neatly finished it off with her short sword.

Botreg had disappeared in the dark and began using his trained assassin skills slipping up behind the Illanni to dispatch them one by one.

All throughout the cavern similar individual battles were going on while Celedant and Inwe made their way to where the spell caster had been. Crouching down, they saw its clothes still alight from Celedant's attack. As the wizard and sorceress neared, it looked up and drew back its teeth to reveal the long incisors of a vampire.

Before it could leap at them, both the spell casters leveled their staffs and drew on the energy of the mountain to send strong beams of light at the beast. They both had chosen the same spell, perhaps by accident or perhaps because of their mutual training on Dragon's Isle. The beams cut through the creature and left two deep, charred holes in his chest and the vampire fell backwards. Celedant stepped forward and used his sword to cut the head from the abomination so it would never rise again. It burst into ash before his eyes.

Then a bright flash came from their right as a second mage attacked.

Celedant un-ceremoniously pushed Inwe to the side and impaled the attacking warlock with his sword. The warlock hissed and Celedant knew he was battling another vampire. The adversary slowly took hold of Celedant's sword and pulled himself up the blade. It was halfway up the sword and about to grasp the hilt and Celedant realized he could not cast a spell without being mauled by the vampire. Suddenly his enemy's eyes widened, and its body turned to ash.

Standing behind the vampire was Hority, a great big smile on his face.

Celedant helped Inwe up and apologized for the rough treatment. She brushed him aside with a haughty look in true high elf style.

Meanwhile the rest of the company were in the process of finishing off the other Illanni that had attacked.

Morganna, breathing hard from her own battle, yelled over to Celedant.

"This was a patrol from Illan to rout out the rebels. I'm not sure, though, why they would be this far out from the city."

Hority was in the middle of the chamber sprinkling dust over his head.

"It matters not," he told Morganna. "Clor was with us this day…or is it night? Come! We must go smite more enemies."

He turned and began to walk away, but Botreg grabbed the dusty dwarf and steered him in the other direction. Both of them heard a crunching sound under their boots and looked down to discover that the room's floor was covered with bones.

"Deprahs' work?" Tarquin asked.

"I think not. These bones have been chewed on," Azimuth answered.

Tarquin, already at the exit to the room, called back to them.

"Someone or something filled this cave with bones."

Morganna halted the group.

"I would guess we have entered the area claimed by the Deprahs," she said.

Hority looked up bashfully as he was putting a bone into his satchel.

"I intend to study the bone when we camp," he said.

The bone did not give off any smell, so the company allowed the inquisitive dwarf to keep it.

Azimuth bent down and picked up one skull.

"It seems the tastes of these denizens varies greatly. This is a skull of an Illanni." He pointed to another. "There lies the head of a dwarf...picked clean."

"From here on out not a sound," Tarquin said. "I don't want to be eaten."

The others nodded their consent and began following the hewn passage.

Morganna's hand swept across the smooth wall which reminded her of her home as a young child. The walls of her clan hall had been just as smooth but painted a light color. It had been a happy house that is until her father and mother were turned to vampires. She had barely escaped with her life those many years ago. As she had jumped from the highest window of the manor Morganna had locked eyes on her brother and seen the pain he was going through but also a glimmer of hope that she was escaping.

She put these feelings aside as the company ventured onwards. Botreg swore they were going south and the others believed him because of his keen knowledge of tunnels and their ways. They soon came to a portion of tunnel that had strange, small tunnels all along its sides. Tarquin went up to them to get a clearer view.

"These are cleanly delved tunnels. I think we should be extra quiet from now on. I would wager that we are in the domain of the Deprahs"

As they continued down the passage, the dwarves admired the stonework of the Deprahs. The tunnel's sides were smooth to the touch and the delving brought out the colors of the different veins running through the granite.

"This is truly beautiful," Celedant whispered.

Tarquin felt a tug on his cloak, turned and saw Hority with a serious look on his soot stained face.

"This place reeks of evil, Tarquin," Hority said. "There is not a bit of dirt or even dust. It is an abomination to Clor."

The leader patted the dwarf on the shoulder and said to him, "Keep an eye out, then, and be as quiet as you can be."

Several turns of the clock passed and they came to a crossing of tunnels where four separate corridors led off into the darkness. Eldahir, Elanesse and Morganna shook their heads. The passages all appeared empty. They took the left hand tunnel that was going more or less toward Illan and they advanced slowly until they heard a scraping sound that seemed to be paralleling their corridor.

Tarquin and Celedant exchanged looks with Kalsti and Morganna, but the Illanni all shrugged their shoulders, not recognizing the sound.

They next reached an area where strange tunnels began to appear on the walls of the main passage at differing heights. The weird sounds had increased and now echoed down these small tunnels. Tarquin quickly went to one opening and listened at the three-foot hole.

Suddenly he saw a small humanoid creature crawling speedily down the passage.

"Ware the tunnels!" he yelled,

Tarquin backed up and was hit by an iron helm with a sharpened spike sticking out from the top. The spike went past his shoulder, but he was still knocked to the ground. "This little man in plate mail must be a Deprah," he thought.

The small figure straddled Tarquin, his large hammer raised above his head. Tarquin quickly grabbed his dagger and jammed it into the creature's underarm, the only open space in the creature's plate armor. Tarquin caught the weakened hammer blow with his left hand and tossed the creature off his chest.

Standing up, Tarquin saw that the corridor was full of the smaller Deprahs engaging the company. He knocked one away with his sword, but more kept coming.

Celedant was standing in the middle of the fight, plying his staff Forestae right and left, crushing skulls and ribs despite the armor on the little bodies.

The company was in the process of being overwhelmed and Botreg was striking the Deprahs and yelling, "Abominations!"

Kalsti and Morganna stood back to back and fended off the creatures with their swords, clanging off one little creature after another. Tarquin found that by striking them upwards, their helmets would fall off and then he could stab them in the face. Eldahir was dancing circles around the creatures and striking them down with ease. Hority had cried "Foes!" and was once again darting about spinning, weaving, and dispatching Deprahs with ease.

Suddenly a horn was blown and the small Deprahs began backing away, their plate mail covered in blood. They quickly retreated and bounded into to the small tunnels, dragging their wounded with them, until they had all disappeared.

Tarquin's company was left breathing hard from the battle. They looked each other over and saw that apart from several deep bruises from the hammers of the creatures they were all in good shape.

Celedant lifted the helmet and stared at the face and head of one fallen creature that looked like a smaller version of a dwarf. Botreg kicked one dead body.

"Tis not natural," he said. "This must be what remains of the dwarves seeking a passage west."

"Everyone run!" Tarquin called out loudly. "They certainly will be back with more soldiers."

They began running down the corridor. Botreg had a deep bruise to his thigh and could not run at full speed and Eldahir and Hority helped him along.

After running for a quarter turn of the clock they reached a section without any of the small tunnels. They stopped breathing hard and Hority kneeled next to his friend Botreg to look at his injury. Azimuth was nearby watching, just in case the monk made a mistake.

Hority made Botreg remove his pants and Tarquin swore he saw the dwarf blush. There was a nasty bruise on his thigh that caused the dwarf such pain that he could hardly move it. The Clorian went into a trance like state and held his hands above the wound. Slowly a brownish light came from his hands and the healing began as the light flowed over the deep bruise. Soon a dark light withdrew and there was a clean spot where Botreg's wound had been.

"There now. Good as new," Hority told him. "The bone was not broken. Ye was lucky there. It will hurt, but at least ye can run now."

Azimuth slapped the monk on the back, stirring up a small cloud of dirt and dust.

"Well done, young Clorian."

Tarquin smiled as Botreg stumbled around trying to get his pants pulled back up.

"We can heal our minor injuries later," Botreg said. "Be prepared for an attack at any moment. They have fine armor and that can cause us a large problem."

The company made good time along the passage, but they were weary from the chase and the battle. Tarquin kept in front and urged them all onward.

"Once we reach a cavern," he said, "we can stop and rest. If we stop now, we risk the Deprahs catching up with us."

The company took up their pace again and before long Eldahir called out to them.

"We're being followed!"

Celedant called them to a stop and said, "It is time for magic to be used against these pesky villains."

By then they could all hear the pounding of feet and the clanging of armor as the little creatures came running up the passage. Celedant positioned himself several feet in front of the company and began to cast a spell by chanting in an ancient tongue that no one but Eldahir, Inwe and the dragons could understand. His staff became infused with power.

Once the first of the Deprahs could be seen, he let lose the power of his staff and a loud crack could be heard echoing through the tunnel. The company was momentarily blinded. The powerful spell shot down the corridor into the front rows of their enemies and those Deprahs were incinerated with nothing remaining but ash and red-hot plate mail.

The power of the spell expanded outward as it raced down the corridor and created a furnace of the air.

Still the Deprahs came running over their dead and tried to reach the company and crossbow bolts came shooting out from the mass of tiny attackers. The defenders quickly took cover on either side of the passage and lay flat to keep from being injured.

Tarquin and several others stood bravely and started shooting arrows down the hall, but their arrows broke or ricocheted off of the fine plate mail of the Deprahs.

The company all rose then and continued running down the tunnel from the creatures until the passage opened up into a large room. The company ranged themselves around the carved walls of the chamber and waited for their enemies to approach.

The plate mailed creatures ran into the cavern and a confusing battle broke out. The Deprahs, merely three feet tall, could dodge under the blows from their taller opponents and even though several were killed as they entered the room, there were just too many for the company.

The company adjusted how they fought using their weapons to strike downwards onto the heads of the Deprahs in order to send many of the creatures reeling from the battle with head wounds. They also found they could strike the Deprahs with upwards swings to dislodge the helmets from the little creatures before striking their head.

Botreg began calling to them in dwarfish and the Azimuth called out in the ancient langue of the dwarves as well. Several of the Deprahs then stopped fighting and began calling to their compatriots while they backed off from the fight, their weapons still at the ready.

Then company got its first clear look at their attackers.

They were smaller than dwarves, but had beards and the same features as that race, but they had small bones interwoven in their beards and through their noses. They were indeed, the long-lost dwarves that had sought a passage to the south and west and were now known as Deprahs.

Azimuth began a clipped conversation with the one he thought could have been their leader. Ash covered his face and there were many bones in his beard that Azimuth could hear rattling against on his plate mailed chest.

Botreg translated for the others what the leader of the Deprahs said to Azimuth.

"They say we are trespassing on their hunting grounds and that we owe them one member of our group as compensation."

Hidden behind Inwe and Tarquin, Celedant began casting a spell while he motioned to Azimuth to keep up the conversation.

The dragon spoke a long time with the Deprahs until the chief started rattling the bones on his armor.

"Canna understand a word they are a saying," Hority whispered to Botreg. A tight squeeze on the shoulder by Botreg quieted the dwarf.

Azimuth turned to the others.

"They are adamant that they take one of us for food. Celedant, if you could so kind as to finish your spell before this turns into a blood bath..."

Celedant stepping between Inwe and Azimuth.

"Hold your breath!" he yelled as a fog like substance rolled from the tip of his staff.

The smoke engulfed the Deprahs and the company heard the plate mail starting to strike the floor.

They started running toward the exit, but Hority stopped and took a deep breath and dropped down asleep. Azimuth was closest to him and snatched him up and hoisted him over his shoulder. Dust emerged from the dwarf with each step the transformed dragon took.

They all ran for what seemed like ages and then slid to a halt when they came to the end of the delved passages and came into a rough cavern. They stopped and Hority began coughing and sat up from the floor where Azimuth had deposited him.

Celedant stood over him.

"That was a most foolish thing to do, young Hority. Suppose that had been a killing cloud. You would be dead now. Then what would Clor do? You're a fool of a monk."

Hority was taken aback.

"I just wanted to see what it smelled like for future reference," he muttered, "and to send a warning back to Clor's valley."

Botreg clouted him on the head.

"The middle of a battle is not the time for experiments," he said and clouted him again.

CHAPTER FIFTEEN

His posture stately and composed, General Maglar Meneldure walked up the stairs of the temple. He had an audience with Tibersu.

Though he was cautious around his leader, the general of the army would not deign himself to be seen running to his leader's every beck and call, but word had just reached him from orc scouts that a wood and high elven army had entered the underworld and were advancing upon Illan.

The vampire guards along the way, dressed in full plate armor, came to attention as he passed. His reputation as a harsh commander preceded him.

He found Tibersu sitting at a table in a side room of the temple. The leader could blend into the darkness easily enough, except that the general's eyes were adapted to the pitch-black inkiness. The general stood at attention by the door until his lord motioned him in.

Maglar sat at the opposite end of the table from Tibersu.

"The elves are advancing toward Illan, my lord," the general said.

The other Illanni hissed and showing his fangs.

"Do you not think I know this already?" Tibersu asked.

The general's lips twitched and briefly showed the elongated teeth of a vampire.

"I understand, my lord."

"How do you plan to deal with this incursion?" asked the ruler of the Illanni.

"The great cavern Docuser lies along their route. I plan to confront them there. In fact, already small forces of ours are nibbling at their heels as they advance." He dared not say that these attacks were being easily repulsed or that only those led by a vampire had succeeded in causing harm to the elven column. The general continued, "They sap the strength of the elves by wounding and killing their scouts. The column has to stop and deal with their dead and wounded."

Tibersu hissed again sharply.

"Can you defeat the ground elves?" he asked.

Maglar sat up sharply before he spoke.

"I can and will. I have vampires leading each company and the rank and file will fight for them. They will fear their commanders more than their foes, and they will fight. I have about a thousand of our best fighters and three thousand orcs and their ilk. The elves should be outnumbered, and we shall defeat them and harry them back to the surface world."

"Good," Tibersu said. "We can't let them threaten our progress to save our people. My wife will not have died in vain. My grand plan will continue, and our dominance will be complete."

He cared not a whit about his wife's death anymore, but leaned on the tragedy to spur on his subordinates. Tibersu had been using it to gain popularity and sympathy amongst the vampires and Illanni ever since his wife had died.

•　　　•　　　•　　　•　　　•

As the elven army marched along the passage, smaller tunnels branched out from the main corridor and from these the Illanni constantly attacked in small groups. They would use the darkness and wait well-hidden because they knew that at each such passage their hated cousins would send a small force to try to clear the area.

As they moved up the tunnels, the Illanni would attack the scouts of the elvan army sent to gather information, but these were quick engagements and normally involved a few arrows shot from the dark. When a vampire was leading the Illanni, though, an all-out fight would ensue. The dark elves would charge forward, led by the vampire, and the battle would start.

Then, in the never-ending darkness of the underworld, swords would clash, and battle cries would be heard. The Illanni were equal to their above ground cousins, but the vampires could use their supreme physical attributes to toss about the wood elves and high elves. They would be thrown down by the vampire and crash against the tunnel's rocky floor. It usually took four elves of light to surround the vampire and eventually decapitate it by using their skilled sword play.

Often, though, the vampire and the Illanni would just withdraw from their attack after a quick skirmish.

The casualties were mounting and keeping the clerics busy while slowing down the column and bleeding it dry. The elves began sending wizards with the scouts that explored the side passages and they would try and to pinpoint the vampires' locations and incinerate the foul creatures before they could initiate battle. The vampires themselves had innate magical abilities, though, and a war of magic would break out at a moment's notice. When it did, the Illanni would withdraw and the elves of light would retreat a short distance back into the tunnel.

General Orthorion called a meeting after the first of the attacks and summoned two of his captains.

"Arantir and Trimimar," he said, "I have a mission for you. These assaults by the Illanni cannot be allowed to happen with such frequency. We are losing too many soldiers…both dead and wounded. I want you two to take over these skirmishes and command of the rear guard and see if you cannot slow these assaults."

The captains nodded in unison as they accepted the command and they immediately turned and ran towards the rear of the advancing elvish army.

As the two captains ran, they heard a commotion down one of the side tunnels and saw in it a large fire pit surrounded by minotaurs and their families. The elves had stumbled onto a home of the monsters with their huge muscled bodes and bull like heads with long horns to match. They had been warned of differing monsters that lived in the underworld, but luckily they had only stumbled upon this small den of the great brutes.

As they advanced cautiously by, a body came hurtling from the camp and a wood elf landed next to the two captains. The elf had his head crushed in and Trimimar ordered the elves to fall back. He hoped the minotaurs would stay in their den once they realized an army was marching nearby.

Instead, several of the huge monsters came out from their den to follow them. They wielded great stone axes, and the wood elves fired arrows at the behemoths and penetrated the thick hide of the creatures. Wounded, and not too happy about the arrows in them, they charged into the elves and swung their axes to clear their way.

The minotaurs waded through the elves and used both their axes and their horns as weapons. Bending low, they would hook an elf with their horn and toss him into the air while at the same time using their axes to beat aside the elves' shields. Many of the two captains' soldiers were falling away wounded and many others lay at the feet of the monsters.

Arantir and Trimimar knew they had to close with the creatures and get inside the swinging axes if they were to pull off a successful attack. Arantir leaped over one low swing from a minotaur while Trimimar rolled up so close to the feet of another minotaur that the beast could only use its horns. Arantir then found himself right next to the creature and rammed his sword up under the rib cage and deep into its chest to piece its great heart.

Trimimar saw that his opponent was now stooping to gore him with its horn, but with a quick swing, his sword stopped the blow from the horn before it reached him cutting the horn off the head of the minotaur.

With a great roar, the monster pulled in its arms and pinned Trimimar to its body. The elf felt the air leaving his body and the pain of his ribs beginning to give way. He desperately struck upwards with his sword. The weapon went under the creature's jaw and into its brain and the elf captain felt the pressure release from his arms. The minotaur fell backwards.

Arantir was there in an instant to pull the minotaur's arms from Trimimar's body.

They both were shaking and shocked at the amount of elven bodies that now lay in a circle around the dead creatures. The elves lying at the feet of the minotaurs were moaning in pain and the two captains quickly began handing them off to other elves to be taken to the healers. Five lay dead, though, and with shaking arms the captains picked the bodies up and carried them back to the elven column.

• • • • •

The company progressed down the passage four several turns of the clock until they heard the unmistakable sound of water. Morganna slowed the column down and explained what that meant to them.

"This is the territory of the Ickthus. They live in the water and I can definably say they eat people such as us, especially those who stray too close to their lairs. We must be quiet and not touch the water. They will be able to feel the disturbance through the lake."

They advanced until the passage opened up to their right and a great lake appeared, its shores running off in front of them along the side of the water. Morganna pointed to the water and shook her head.

"Hority! Heed my warning!" she added sternly.

The cleric drew near the lake, but after hearing her words, he slunk back to the company, helped along by a quick jerk on his shirt collar by Botreg.

The party of adventurers continued along, keeping the lake to their side, and suddenly they could hear splashes off in the distance where several natural pathways disappeared into the darkness of the lake.

Morganna put her finger to her mouth and told the others to be quiet as they passed the dark walkways. In the distance they could see fire light across the lake.

"Probably a small settlement," Morganna whispered, "We must be extra careful."

Their passageway ended and they saw a fissure that split the passage in half and allowed the water to fill the void. It looked too far to jump across and Morganna looked upwards, as if she were asking, "Why can nothing be easy about this journey?"

Tarquin came forward and took a long look at the water that flooded the passage. He turned to the others.

"The fissure is about twenty paces across," he whispered. "I'm afraid it's too far for most of us to jump."

They all stood and stared at the fissure.

"There is no telling its depth," Inwe said, "and the space here is too small for a dragon to morph without disturbing the water. We—I mean the elves—would have no problem jumping the water. However, the burden of an extra body would be too much. So that leaves the others stranded and our mission in jeopardy."

Celedant spoke the thought that was occurring in the minds of the others.

"The elves can jump across the ravine. I can levitate the rest across."

"I can carry little Hority and make the jump," Azimuth stated.

The golden dragon Azimuth stared out at the dark lake while the elves jumped the distance and the others were teleported across.

Azimuth, Celedant's lifelong friend, grasped the dwarf Hority under the armpits and in a few bounds soared across the crevasse. They didn't notice that the filthy dwarf's satchel was jostled by the jump and Hority's precious collection was almost lost as it turned sideways. Unfortunately for the group, a rock the monk had intended to study fell to plop into the water far below.

After they had all landed safely, Celedant whispered urgently to them, "I can feel we're being watched."

Morganna and Kalsti yelled, "Ickthus!"

Suddenly the water along the shore erupted with pale white, fish-like beings. They looked ill formed, their heads fish-shaped but cantered forward like the face of a human. They had fin like arms and legs that were heavily muscled and ended in webbed fingered hands and toes. Their tails were wide and flat, and they had pink eyes that saw perfectly in the near darkness of their cavern.

They carried nets and tridents and immediately threw the nets at the company. Tarquin was caught in one, but as the Ickthus neared him, he leaped forward and drove his dagger deep into the creature's chest.

The creatures stood man height and Tarquin could not see how his companions were doing until he cut himself out from the netting. He immediately had to dodge a trident, but he then grasped it and pulled the creature onto his sword. Another Ickthus was climbing out from the fissure and Tarquin gave him a quick kick in the face before turning to help the others.

Tarquin started working his way down the passage, fighting and killing as he went. He chopped and thrust his way forward, freeing his friends from the combat and allowing several of his band to disentangle themselves from the netting. They followed him when a second wave of Ickthus came screaming out of the water.

He and the others turned quickly to parry the enemy's tridents and dodge their nets. Tarquin and his company began to strike back at the Ickthus and soon the water was turning red and the passageway had become slick with blood.

Hority lay against the wall and held his thigh where a trident had struck him. He saw Celedant and the other magic wielders striking back from the front of their company. Their bright lights shot high into the air and blinded their enemies. The Ickthus were used to fire, but the extreme brightness of the energy spells was something they had never experienced. Celedant and his fellow magic wielders directed other spells at the Ickthus which wounded them or killed them outright.

Other enemy warriors were still issuing forth from the water, but the magic wielders' balls of magic shot out from the dry passage and kept many of the Ickthus at bay.

Tarquin dodged another trident and smashed the pommel of his sword into the creature's face. Its bones crushed; the creature dove back into the water. All along the passageway the weaker Ickthus began to dive into the water. They had had enough of the fight, but some of the larger ones still dueled with Tarquin's company.

Eldahir and one of the monstrous creatures went toe to toe, back and forth between the wall and water, until the elf sliced an arm off his enemy. The he cut across the body of the Ickthus and sliced through its throat. Eldahir kicked it in the chest and it fell back into the water.

Once that monstrous Ickthus died, the other Ickthus lost heart and followed behind their champion back into the water.

Azimuth used his dragon like strength to break off the trident's tine that was stuck through Hority's leg and he pulled the weapon out of him. He quickly picked up the barely conscious dwarf and, with Morganna in the lead, the company all ran to find somewhere to treat Hority's wound.

They reached the end of the lake and, with Tarquin guarding the rear of the company and Azimuth the front, the company stopped in the dry passage to see to Hority and their other wounded. Most of them had bruises from tridents hitting their armor, but Hority lay bleeding on the floor. Morganna sat holding his head while Eldahir cleaned the wound. The trident's tine had passed cleanly through his thigh.

Elanesse came instantly to his side and despite the dwarf's odor, she pulled his habit over Hority's head. In nothing but his filthy loin cloth, the dragon went to work. Rubbing her hands together she began to chant in a language only Azimuth could understand and she took an animal skin full of clean water and pressed the opening into his wound. Still chanting, she squeezed the water flask. At first just dirty, foul water emerged from the wound, but soon it turned clean

She stopped her chant and placed hands on both the entry and exit wound. When Elanesse removed her hands, the wounds were gone. Only small indentations were left. She touched them with her fingers and then looked up at Tarquin.

"By the look of his myriad of other scars," she said. "these will seem insignificant. We should still wrap a tight linen bandage around his leg. He has been healed, but that wound may hurt for several days and impair his mobility."

Hority woke up and smiled at Morganna.

"Clor be praised," he said. "Now that I am healed, we can begin our quest again".

It took him but a single click of the clock to realize that he was missing his habit and with a brightly red face, he snatched it from Morganna and turned his back to her as he slipped it over his head.

•   •   •   •   •

When Arantir and Trimimar had joined the rear guard, they had commanded that after each attack from a side passage, the wood and high elvan troops should fall to the rear while fresher troops would see to the nearest passage.

As planned, the elves who had just returned from a side passage had to take up positions as the newest rear guard, but they would still have to watch their backs in case the Illanni attacked.

After one fierce battle in a side tunnel, the rear guard was attacked. The Illanni had used the battle in the side tunnel to mask their other movements. Although most of the elves' eyes had been drawn to what was becoming a large battle in the side passage, more elves were ordered back down the column to support the rear guard when arrows started to fly into those troops by the hundreds.

Many were wounded and tried to drag themselves behind boulders and as the elves of light sent more soldiers to the rear, the Illanni attacked in earnest. Elves of light fired their bows in response and many of the dark ones fell, wounded or dead.

The two new captains began shouting orders as they bravely stood out in the open, not cowering behind cover. Their courage and élan kept the wood elves and high elves attacking and their wizards unleashed fireball spells to stop the Illanni advancing up the tunnel. Powerful blocking spells were then cast by the enemy's warlocks and the elves and the dark ones charged at one another and clashed fiercely in the depth below the earth's surface.

The elves of light vaulted over boulders and rocks to engage the Illanni and the lifelong hatred and mistrust between the two spurred on their battle lust. Arrows from both sides shot through the others' attacking forces and precisely struck one elf or Illanni after another.

Suddenly, five great cave giants over five cubits tall, in full chain mail and wielding great swords, began wading through the Illanni. Elven arrows bounced off their chainmail or stuck into their skin, but the giants hardly seemed to notice it.

The two captains of the wood and high elf army were exquisite in their swordsmanship, but still many wounded elves were carried back to the clerics that waited behind the engagement. The battle front had turned into a complete melee as the two forces intertwined, and there were no longer any battle lines as there had been at the onset of the attack. It was kill or be killed. Wizards and warlocks battled while vampires stalked the battlefield, grabbing wood elves and high elves and hoisting them up from behind. These elves tried to fight the vampires, but soon their throats were ripped open by the thirsty creatures.

Meanwhile, the giants swung their great swords effectively and cut down elves of all sides as if they were wheat. These huge monsters would not retreat. Fired by their own blood lust, they steadily advanced into the midst of the elves of light.

Many elves would stand on boulders and launch themselves at the vampires and as they flew by them in the air, slice off their heads, turning them into dust. Meanwhile the sheer number of the elves of light began to take its toll on the Illanni assault. A horn was blown behind the Illanni and those that could began to retreat. Those Illanni who were still locked in life or death struggles stayed and fought their enemies.

The elves of light advanced, but they were still slowed to a halt from the many arrows that came from the retreating dark ones. They replied and between these last two arrow barrages, the final few fights took place. The elven victor of these one on one combats would hunch over behind a boulder while if the dark Illanni won they would run for its life in the direction of their retreating comrades.

The giants were more difficult to deal with and the smaller elves had to retrieve large spears from their stores and advance on the huge creatures. With their longer pikes, the elves could stay well enough away from the giants' great swords while the elves pikes' sharpened tips easily penetrated the giants' chain mail armor.

Soon all five were down on the ground and were being finished off by the elves.

The final barrage of arrows petered out and the dark ones withdrew and left the battlefield to the wood and high elves. The wood elves began a sweep of the area to make sure the dark ones were truly dead, not just wounded. Their own wounded and dead were carefully carried back to elven lines.

Desecrating the body of another being was considered by the elves to be one of the worst crimes one could commit so the elves killed by the vampires were gently returned to their battle lines while the wounded vampires themselves all had to be beheaded and turned to ash. The wounded Illanni would fight back when they were found and swift little battles would take place as these Illanni were dealt with. After each short duel to the death a few more of the elves of light were left wounded or dead.

Arantir and Trimimar, the two leaders of the rear guard, saw their many dead being carried to the sides of the tunnel. Without thinking they picked up the body of one dead wood elf lying at their feet, the first of the many gruesome tasks that the two captains had to carry out. They both had tears streaming down their faces as they lay the last body down.

All the remaining elves that the captains had commanded bowed heads in silence to mourn the comrades they had lost in the battle.

Word of the attack had reached Orthorion several clicks of the clock after the battle had begun. He wished he had been there to command the forces, but he had to rely on his personally picked captains. He had ordered from afar the elven column to take a defensive position where they were, but afterward he could only await the news from the rearguard.

The report came and it was not good news. So many elves had been wounded, they were overtaxing the clerics and their healing abilities. A fair number of elves had also died, but more dark elves had been killed and Orthorion, hearing this news, bowed his head. He dreaded how many more of his command would die in the coming days.

He was beginning to rethink his whole battle plan. Had he taken too few soldiers? Should he had left the venture to Morganna and her company?

He had rarely had second thoughts about war, but this last horrid battle was now slowly sinking into his gut.

CHAPTER SIXTEEN

Morganna and Kalsti believed they were now near the city of Illan, but still too far away to encounter any of the resistance. The tunnels had narrowed and were closing in on them and the boulders once again blocked their way and gave them a difficult time while crawling over them. It was a terrain that ached to sprain an ankle or break a leg.

They turned a corner in the tunnel and heard off-key singing in the distance and saw the light from a flickering fire. The company quickly took cover behind the boulders in the tunnel.

"Botreg, go see what this is all about," Tarquin ordered.

Botreg looked at his former Borderer commander and said, "Thanks for volunteering me, again...even though we are not in the Borderers any longer."

The former assassin, dressed all in black, disappeared in the blink of an eye as he crawled forward. Botreg could see the light clearly after a hundred feet. More ominously, he saw many large shadows moving about in a cavern and he crawled further ahead to get a better look at what he realized were a mixture of oversized humans and goblins. The goblins were dancing around a fire pit while the humans laughed and sang.

Botreg stayed there, watching and listening, for a quarter turn of the clock.

He watched a human stand, stretch in an odd way, drop to the floor and transform into a werewolf. Standing, it advanced toward the fire. The smaller goblins scattered, but one was not fast enough and was grabbed by the foot. The werewolf quickly banged the goblin's head against the stone floor and plopped it into the fire, turning it over several times. The werewolf bit a huge hunk of meat from the goblin's leg once it had been cooked enough.

In the meantime, another werewolf had crawled through a hole in the low ceiling of the cave and landed amongst its kin. The men about the fire greeted the newcomer in a series of yelps and snarls.

Botreg decided he had seen enough and returned to the company. Crawling out of the dark he surprised several who drew their swords on him.

"What did you see?" Tarquin asked.

The dwarf explained the situation in the cavern.

"I don't think we need to worry about the goblins. They may end up being our allies. But they do block our passage and we must advance."

Tarquin looked around at the others.

"Don't count on those goblins seeing us as rescuers."

The company moved forward, not daring to make a noise by tripping on any rocks, although they thought the singing they heard ahead would probably negate any noise. They neared the opening and drew their bows and notched arrows.

Celedant crawled forward.

"Hold!"

The wizard started chanting under his breath and finished by flicking his arm straight at the werewolves. There was a flash of smoke and out of thin air, four mountain trolls appeared in the middle of the cavern. The other creatures, unsure of what was happening, were taken unawares as the trolls attacked them. A melee quickly broke out the between the tall thin werewolves, who were slightly bigger than the trolls, but the latter had sharpened, yellow brown teeth and long claws.

The werewolves battled the trolls by battering them down with clubs while the trolls quickly jumped onto the werewolves and attacked like feral beasts. Once the attackers seemed to be killed, the first troll to fall rose up to attack again.

One of the brighter humans called out, "Bring fire! That will put an end to these scum."

By the time they had their torches lit, all the trolls had regenerated from their wounds and were back attacking the werewolves.

Celedant patted Tarquin on the back and he sent an arrow though one human's eye. Then the others let fly. Arrows either struck, missed, bounced off the stone of the cave or penetrated the thick hide of the werewolves and dropped them where they stood.

The humans were quickly transforming into their true form of werewolves. When they saw their fallen comrades, they thought they had been killed by the trolls, but as suddenly as the trolls had materialized in midair, they had disappeared. The werewolves realized that they were under attack by someone else.

While the projectiles continued to fly toward them, they turned around for a precious few clicks of the clock while they tried to decide where the arrows were coming from.

Several more werewolves then jumped down through the hole in the ceiling and they were being followed by several dozen goblins. The goblins turned on the werewolves with crude weapons.

Tarquin vaulted out of the cave onto one human's back and thrust with all his might. His sword Dragon Bolt burned bright red as it penetrated the man's head went right through the brain. By then all his company had charged from the cave and were attacking the werewolves and fighting side by side with the goblins out of necessity.

Botreg jumped on one's back and was promptly thrown off to land amid the goblins. He had both his sword and dagger out, but the goblins ignored him as they rushed their oppressors. Ress's spear got stuck between the thick ribs of one of the creatures and the shaft bent and was ready to break when Inwe vaulted by and sliced through its throat.

The goblins swarmed over their enemies with their axes and small swords rising and falling. Soon the werewolves were all dead except for the largest, probably the clan leader. It had jumped up to the hole in the ceiling and was trying to pull itself up, but the goblins were holding tightly on to its feet. Hority was at the bottom, trying to attack the hanging ogre, but his branch was too short to reach the foot. It did, however kill, several goblins by accident.

Finally, the werewolf let go and fell back into the cave. It fell directly onto Hority and his branch finally touched its intended target. Ress was immediately at the side of the creature and she pulled the monster upwards. Botreg pulled the monk by his feet out from under the beast.

Hority was coughing and drawing in great gulps of pure air while Botreg wiped his hands on his cloak, which now reeked of the foul smells of Hority.

"I wish Baldo was here to take care of ye, besides just me," the dark dwarf complained,

A soon as all the werewolves had fallen, the goblins quickly gathered to one side of the cavern. Tarquin's company stood ready for battle, the fire pit separating the two sides, and both groups had their weapons ready and expected the other to attack.

Celedant stepped forward and spoke to the goblins in their own language.

"We mean you no harm. We had a common enemy. Now they are dead. All we wish is to pass through this place and continue on our way."

A large goblin stepped forward.

"Why not you kill us?"

"Because we are friends who fought a common enemy," replied Celedant. "We have destroyed the werewolves. Might I ask for a truce?"

The goblin's brow furrowed, and he had a questioning look on his face. He cocked his head.

"We know not this word," he said.

"It means we won't hurt you," Celedant said, "and you won't hurt us. Until we part ways from one another."

The large goblin spat on the corpse of one werewolf.

"We agree," he said.

"We look for a tunnel out of this place," the wizard said to him.

The goblin nodded.

"There are two tunnels above. Come. I show it to you."

The goblins scaled the rough walls of the cavern and climbed quickly through the hole in the roof of the cave.

Celedant looked at the others.

"I thought to glean information," he said, "without causing a full-scale battle. Come. I'll go first."

He took a stout rope from Eldahir and with a single word levitated upwards and through the hole. The rope dropped, and the others climbed up. The only one to complain was Hority, who distrusted the rope because it was so clean.

The company found themselves in a small cavern with two tunnels. The goblins were nowhere to be seen. Their truce had not lasted long, but it was long enough.

Morganna was inspecting the two passages.

"This one the goblins fled through," she said. "This other has not had traffic through it in many years. Also, I can smell fresh air coming from the passage the goblins took."

Celedant walked toward the other passage.

"Come now!" he said to the company. "Why do we wait?"

CHAPTER SEVENTEEN

The company started off down the smooth passage that now felt much safer than the many miles they had spent crawling over the boulders that had been dislodged from the passage's ceiling. They traveled for two days before a vast cavern opened up in front of them.

Morganna halted them.

"There is something wrong here," she said. "I can feel it."

"Well guessed," a voice called out from the darkness.

The company all tensed, drew their weapons and turned to where the voice had come from. The voice continued.

"Morganna. It has been a long time, but I remember your voice well enough."

"Who are you? Show yourself," she yelled and her words echoed throughout the cave.

The mysterious voice said, "It is I, Dinendal, your old friend."

Morganna and Kalsti smiled. They had stumbled across an old friend of theirs and they stepped out of the tunnel to greet the figure now emerging from around a large boulder.

They all embraced.

"Everyone! This is an old friend and comrade in the fight to end Illan's tyranny," Morganna said. "Dinendal can be trusted."

Hority leaned towards Celedant, who bent low to hear the whispering dwarf.

"I don't trust chance meetings," Hority said.

"Humm. I don't either," Celedant whispered back. "We best be ready. Best for you to venture forth to the head of the company."

The company was then surrounded by twenty other smiling Illanni, all eager to greet Morganna and Kalsti back among their midst.

Dinendal was still hugging Kalsti, but then he reared back and showed the fangs of a vampire. Suddenly he ripped Morganna's closest friend's throat out.

He turned and called out to the others behind him.

"Kill the traitors!"

Suddenly what had begun as a reunion turned into a full-fledged battle. Arrows flew from the Illanni, catching the company unaware, and Celedant was thrown backwards. Both Inwe and Elanesse went down under the barrage of arrows that had been aimed specially at the magic users. Eldahir stood firm and sent arrow after arrow into the attackers while Tarquin charged the archers, his sword drawn. Behind him he heard the unmistakable battle cry of "Foes!" in Hority's distinctive voice.

Arrows were still flying as Tarquin turned and ran into several of the Illanni. The first one he struck down quickly with a deep slash across his chest and he dueled with the other before finishing him off with Dragon Bolt burning bright.

Tarquin quickly ran on while Hority danced out of way of the arrows and brought down an Illanni with his pumice topped branch.

Morganna stepped over Kalsti, her lifelong friend, and attacked Dinendal. As they dueled, they continued to probe each other's sword work, both on the defensive and offensive, and after several rounds of attacking and defending, Morganna saw a weakness. When she did, her warrior's madness overtook her and she struck the sword hand from her attacker with the flat of her blade. His sword fell to the floor of the cave and he stood there, surprised.

Morganna then neatly severed his head and turned him into ashes.

Botreg knew that the remaining attackers would try to escape so he dodged his way to the back of the cave to the passage leading out. One Illanni had beaten him there, but the dark dwarf drew two daggers and threw them at the fleeing dark elf. The daggers took the Illanni in the middle of the back and the back of the thigh. He was still trying to crawl away when Botreg kneeled on his back and slit his throat.

Without their leader the remaining Illanni had formed a defensive position behind boulders and had begun shooting arrows every time a members of the company moved. Botreg saw his friends pinned down by the enemy and began stealthily moving behind the Illanni. Eldahir sent his arrows with unerring aim after each Illanni exposed itself and he watched as several of the dark ones spun around, his arrows embedded in their bodies.

Meanwhile, the former assassin had moved behind the Illanni and quickly began to dispatch them with his sword and dagger, but suddenly an arrow splintered against a rock just above his head.

"Eldahir! Tarquin! It's me, Botreg," he called out.

He continued onward and killed the last of the enemy.

The company waited a good half a turn of the clock to make sure they had killed all the Illanni and Botreg crawled back to the exit of the cave to kill anyone that still tried to escape.

•   •   •   •   •

The Illanni had been taken care of. It was time to see to the company's wounds.

Kalsti was dead. There was nothing that could be done for her, but to shield Morganna from what happened next, Botreg dragged Kalsti's body behind some boulders to decapitate her. She was so newly dead that the vampire disease had not started to spread throughout her body, and she did not turn to ash. With the help of a praying Hority, Botreg began building a cairn over the body.

Morganna was inconsolable and Eldahir held her tightly. The members of the company sought out the rest of the Illanni and decapitated them, just in case they had been turned.

Hority, the monk of Clor, saw to the High Elf and to Elanesse.

"Leave me be," the dragon said haughtily to the monk. "I'll heal in time. See to my bond mate."

Hority went over to Inwe, who had an arrow straight through her chest. Hority tsk-tsked,

"Tis not deep," he said. "I will pray to Clor for your healing."

He then sat beside her and gently grasped the arrow with his hand. Ever so slowly he broke the arrowhead that stuck a few inches out of her back and pulled the projectile from her chest. He closed the wound in a cloud of brown dust.

He then gathered a vial of her blood and she gave him a quizzical stare.

"I have never examined elf blood," he explained, "and deem this an excellent chance."

Morganna was still broken from her sorrow and she spoke absently.

"We need to move. Others probably heard this battle."

The battered company then took the passage out of the cavern at a steady run.

Morganna weakly called back to them

"I know these passages. We are close to Illan."

She spotted a small, nearly invisible print on the wall and held up her hand, pointing to it for the others to see.

"There is one of our hidden signs," she said. "Come quickly. There must be a camp nearby."

She led them at a fast pace as she followed the signs on the wall. Finally, she stopped and called out.

"It is Morganna. I am sorry, but there may be Illanni behind us."

Twenty rebel Illanni appeared out of thin air.

"Morganna," their leader said. "It is good to see you, my friend."

Theiors, a commander in the underground movement, breathed a sigh of relief.

"We thought you might be something attacking us," he said. "We could hear you a mile away. Come here. It is a precaution, but we must see your teeth."

Morganna's friends allowed them to check their teeth even though Inwe was reluctant until Celedant persuaded her. Then the underground Illanni showed the company their own teeth.

"We encountered a patrol with Dinendal as their leader," Morganna informed the underground leader. "He had been turned, but you need not worry about him anymore."

The underground commander shook his head back and forth.

"I was afraid that had happened. He was weeks behind returning to our territory. That means we must leave here immediately just in case he told the vampires of our hiding place.

The dark ones fanned out to cover both their front and back flanks and they continued ever deeper into the mountain and down a carved passageway. Finally, Theiors motioned for them all to stop.

"Welcome to your new home…for the time being. We still have to move every so often to avoid attacks by the vampires. But this is our base for the time being even though we must move again immediately."

The Illanni rebels settled into a cave with cavities cut in the limestone walls. Morganna was welcomed by all there, but the loss of Kalsti struck the whole community with sadness. She had been one of the Illanni who had engineered their original uprising. Several dark ones openly wept and had to be consoled by their friends.

All the while the rebel Illanni were packing up their belongings.

Theiors took Morganna and Celedant aside.

"The Illanni have been sending regular patrols, accompanied by vampires," he said. "We move our location every seven days. It was just luck that you found us here at all."

Morganna asked, "Might we continuing speaking to you...in private?"

The Illanni bowed. "But of course."

He led them toward a far doorway.

"You have curious friends," he said to Morganna. "Humans, wood elves, high elves and dwarves. If I had seen them before I saw you, I might have attacked. You never know who the vampires will have under their control these days."

They entered a small barren room and Theiors motioned with outstretched arms.

"A quiet place to talk," he said. "I know it's not just friendship that brings you back to our lovely city."

"No," Morganna said. "We have come to strike at the heart of the vampires. At my father, to be precise."

Elves seldom made facial expressions, but Theiors' face showed his shock.

"That is not something undertaken haphazardly," he said.

"No, it is not," agreed Morganna, "but it could very well spell these vampires' downfall. General Orthorion has marched into the underworld with an army of elves bent on striking at the city."

The other rebel Illanni nodded.

"We knew that there were surface dwellers running amok in the tunnels. It has the vampires and their soldiers very upset. It was like someone kicked over an anthill several days ago when those Illanni exited the city marching north."

"It is urgent," Morganna said in a serious voice. "And I need a message delivered."

Theiors asked, "To whom do you need this message to go? I can arrange it."

"You might want to reconsider before readily accepting my plea," Morganna said. "I need it to go to Boltrein, my brother."

Theiors looked askance.

"You would be announcing yourself to the vampires that you are here. You might as well stand in the great square and blow a trumpet. He is the son…just as are you the disgraced daughter of Tibersu, as you well know."

Morganna's hard voice came back at him.

"Yes, I am his sister. I know my brother. He will not betray me. Our bond is strong. He will come despite his condition. I have no fear, but we will take precautions."

Theiors looked down at the granite floor for a brief click of the clock.

"I can get a message to him," he said. "That's the easy part. The hard part is preparing for his arrival."

"My old quarters will suit," Morganna said. They're in the perfect area for us to be prepared for any unwanted guests."

"Alright," said Theiors. "This is against my better judgment, but I will do it for you."

CHAPTER EIGHTEEN

The Illanni General Maglar Meneldure strode out of the temple thinking that his lord Tibersu was getting madder each day. At least for now the general had a mission to do, though, and he could leave all these other machinations to those higher up the chain of command.

The army had assembled, and he made his way to the head of the dark elf soldiers. As he passed the foremost Illanni, he uttered not a word yet the column followed. The Illanni beat a quiet cadence on a drum and several horns announced the column to move out, but their orcan allies made enough noise to wake the dead. This was not lost on the general and he smiled at the thought of the pending battle.

They would lose many of their orcan allies, but that did not worry the general. Fodder was fodder, and as long as they stayed, he had a better chance at stopping the incursion. There was a finite number of invaders and he could summon more allies if he needed them. The initial reports on the attack on the elves of light were encouraging. His smaller forces had stood up well to the elves, and many of the enemy had been wounded and their death toll was high.

There were four passages that led to the cavern of Docuser and the Illanni made use of all four. They were a mixed army with Illanni fighting alongside both orcs and the occasional ogre. General Maglar felt the orcs would be bolstered by his troops even though they were downright scared of the Illanni they were fighting alongside, not to mention the vampires sent to herd them along.

The orcs were issued the order to keep quiet under pain of death and they advanced slowly up the passages, not wanting any elf scout to hear them.

The passage they were on slowly opened up into the giant cavern of Docuser that ran east to west, not that that even mattered so deep in the earth. Maglar had his forces fanned out along the southern portion of the giant cave and with their backs against the wall of the cavern, he knew there could be no retreat.

The cavern's ceiling arched up past where the dark elves could see. The floor of the cavern was relatively smooth because the ancient river that had formed the cavern had left the floor void of the rock formations and boulders that littered most other caves. Maglar noted a small rivulet still flowed in a meandering way across the cave.

•   •   •   •   •

Boltrein had heard the stirrings of the army long before the general had seen Tibersu. His informants had told him that the dark elves would march out of the city within a turn of the clock. Then there came a great blowing of horns and deep pounding of a single drum as the army began its march.

He stood at the window of his study trying to think through the different scenarios that could happen. Morganna was cautious and would not advance with the Wood and High elvan army. It all fit with her tactics leading the rebellion. She was an expert at moving in small groups and picking off dark elf patrols as they moved frightened Illanni through the underworld.

Morganna would be treading this way with a small group. They would be well used to the dark tunnels of the underground and be powerful enough to withstand the terrors that lurked in the darkness. They would move fast and with her contacts with the underground could already be nearby. Boltrein knew her end game would be the death of their father.

Though sickened by Tibersu's rule and the fact that he had been attacked by an assassin most likely sent by his father Boltrein still had deep feelings for the plight his people. Tibersu had begun to save his race. The power of the vampires had indeed turned the tide in the underworld. The Illanni could safely navigate the twisting passages of the ever dark.

Was he ultimately loyal to his race as directed by his father true to his vampire's blood? However, there was a deep part of him a non-vampiric part of his soul that disagreed with that question. He had been forced into his current state and saw too many of his comrades of the clans turned against their will. That deep part of his psyche cheered on his sister and increased his love of her.

CHAPTER NINETEEN

General Orthorion had prepared for Illanni attacks along the tunnel the army now traveled. He had placed two of his finest captains in charge of the rear of the column and he trusted those two elves to manage any attacks. The general knew he could not leave a force of elves at every tunnel they came across or he would sap his army of its strength.

The Illanni still struck all along the column issuing forth from side passages. They were vicious little fights, but where there were no vampires, the Illanni put up token attacks to bleed the column of elves. When there was a vampire or a full-scale battle erupted urged on by the vampires, the small confines of the underworld gave the Illanni the advantage, but the elves adapted well. They suffered little losses, but the number of their wounded continually mounted and that slowed their advance.

Arantir and Trimimar ordered that at each tunnel or passage a small contingent of elves would stand guard as the army passed. This seemed to ease the attacks and if there was one, the elves had enough soldiers in those small spaces to take care of the enemy.

It was the large caverns, though, that the front of the column felt the brunt of the attacks. The Illanni and their minions—mostly orcs and ogres—fought for every foot and the vampires fought even harder, like mad demons recklessly and without fear. Their superior strength gave them a great advantage.

The vampires could be killed by blows to the head and with fire, and the elves found the best way to kill one was to pen it down on the ground and slice the head from the body. In many cases an elven wizard would cast a fire ball spell that incinerated all in its path, including the vampires.

After a while there were no more attacks for some time, and that boded ill to the two captains.

• • • • •

Martish's company was still not up to strength.

She was cautious about who would ride and fight alongside her and although she still only had a little over one hundred soldiers, they were the most experienced warriors she could find. Among the rank and file, it was a considerable accomplishment to be chosen for her elite company, and venturing forth to deal death to the elves of light lit up the imagination of the even the dullest dark elf soldier.

Martish was sitting down amongst her troops and there were only a few of the original fighters left from the battles they had fought.

"If things go badly in the coming engagement," she whispered to her company, "be ready to retreat. If there is a vampire leading our section, I will take care of it. Now rest and sharpen your weapons. Our gear is secreted in the smaller tunnel leading to the surface. Once we reach there, we can see what will be."

A haughty vampire came along and stood next to Martish.

"You will fight like you never have before," it told her. "I will make sure that anyone fleeing the battle will be killed."

Martish, having been around too many vampires, was not affected by his bravado.

"You need not worry about my company," she said. "We will fight the outsiders."

The vampire nodded. "I see no fear in your eyes. Neither I nor the pending fight seem to faze you, captain."

"I am Martish and I have had my share of fighting above ground. I have even taken Tibersu to the home of the wood elves."

The vampire smiled. "I am a different lord then Tibersu. I care not of your past exploits. I should kill you now for being so vain."

Martish kept her hand gripping her new sword hilt. It had yet to reveal its nature, but now might be a good time for her to test it, she thought.

The vampire abruptly turned away and walked over to the orcs that were under his command. He gave them a passing warning and moved on to another unit so he could terrify them, as well, into fighting hard in the coming battle.

•   •   •   •   •

The Illanni general Maglar took a place near the center his lines and sat to wait for the arrival of their enemy. He watched the northern opening for any signs of movement and after several turns of the clock, he thought he saw several darker shadows moving in the northern passage.

He looked about him at the Illanni soldiers with a smile.

"Looks as if they have turned up for the fight," he said.

He knew this would be a proper battle, fought in the darkness of the underworld, where units could stay together as they advanced across the cavern toward their hated cousins.

All along the Illanni lines soldiers stood silently and readied their weapons for the coming conflict.

The elves were allowed to file out of the tunnel and take positions before the Illanni attacked and they cautiously issued forth from the passage and set up their lines of battle. Once they were ready, General Meneldure signaled a horn to be blown for the dark elves to advance.

The Illanni attacked. A hail of arrows shot forth from the Illanni lines and fell from the darkness of the cavern of Docuser. Their feathers made an eerie sound in flight and the first two volleys of arrows cut into the elves and dropped many to the stone floor.

The Illanni charged in complete silence and a third volley of arrows were shot at the elves while a great drum began to beat in order to spur the Illanni and their allies onwards in a straight line towards their hated enemies.

Maglar, caught up in the rush of the first attack, saw the first flights of arrows stream overhead and then a bright tongue of fire lashed out into the ranks and incinerated all in its path. The general cursed Tibersu's name as the fire rushed over him and he screamed as his flesh was roasted inside his armor.

In the massive charge of the armies, none of the Illanni saw that their commander was now nothing but ashes in his own suit of armor.

The two armies clashed into each other in the total darkness of the cavern. Only a few elven bowmen had made it through the passage and so the return volleys affected the enemy little.

The dark ones then came crashing into the elven ranks and the clashing of the swords and shields echoed throughout the cavern. Arrows flew from both sides, taking their toll, and the wounded and the dead were left where they had fallen. The front lines turned into hand to hand combat as one shield wall pushed against another.

More wood elves and high elves exited the tunnel to fight to the death and elven bowmen darted in and out of the crush of attackers and their bows killed off the orcs and their allies from behind their fellow elfin soldiers in the front shield wall.

General Orthorion placed himself in the fiercest of the fighting. He shouldered his way through the front ranks and took the place of a dead elf that had fallen to the ground. He straddled the elf's body and swung his sword left and right to clear the area so that the elven body could be retrieved.

Then he went on the attack. His long straight sword was perfect for this sort of fighting and it darted over his shield into his foes, killing and wounding them. If the enemy in front of him bore a shield, he could attack around its edges and still inflict a grievous wound. He would swing his sword overhand and it would bite down into the metal rimmed shield. As he forced the shield down, he quickly slid the sword across its rim and into the face of his attacker.

One orc was replaced by another and the battle continued, surging back and forth as each side pushed on the other's shield wall and tried to break it. Some orcs jumped over the wall, but they were quickly killed by the waiting elves of light, each elf ready to take the place of a fallen comrade.

There were fiercer battle in the spots where the dark ones or Illanni fought because their weapons were on par with the elves' and they would battle the other to a standstill. Both the elves and the Illanni possessed nearly impenetrable mythril armor and they battered on each other incessantly. Many of the wounded fell down from broken bones rather than from bleeding wounds and even though their armor saved the elves of light from sword cuts, the force of the blows would crush the bones underneath.

The dead and the wounded began piling up on both sides.

Orthorion cleared the space in front of him by slashing two orcs down, but an Illanni appeared and hissed at the general, its long fangs protruding from its upper jaw. With a quickness born of the supernatural, it attacked and Orthorion barely got his shield up in time. The vampire's sword struck down hard on the general and drove him to one knee. The elf managed to regain his footing despite the bloodied stone floor of the cavern and he struck back. The vampire easily parried his blade and the next attack nearly yanked the shield from the general's arm.

He counterattacked by slicing down across the chain mail of the vampire' chest. Its armor stopped the blow, but it caused the creature drop its sword and the vampire began grappling with the general to avoid the elvan sword. Orthorion landed a blow to the vampire's helmet that sent it flying from the creature's head. His adversary was now hurt and Orthorion saw blood coming out from where the helmet had been pounded into the vampire's face.

Swinging his sword above his head, the general stepped forward and threw the Illanni off balance for a just a click of the clock and then he struck at its head. His sword hummed through the air and neatly severed the head from the vampire. It remained upright briefly before bursting into ash and falling to the ground.

The commanders of the rear guard, Arantir and Trimimar, had advanced with their troops after the battle had commenced and they now stood at the mouth of the entrance to Docuser and overlooked the battle. The elves were holding the Illanni to a standstill, but the orcs, by their sheer number, had pushed into the elven line. Leaving a small guard behind, the two captains pointed to the left side of the line where the orcs were battling, and the elves of light quietly slipped from the cave entrance and charged in that direction.

Trimimar was first to reach the battle lines. He shouldered an orc aside, ran him neatly through and went deeper into the melee. His friend came in slightly later and followed in his footsteps. One orc stepped up behind Trimimar and was ready to slice down across the elf's back, but Arantir slashed its hamstrings. As it fell in agony, the elf sent a backhanded blow that decapitated his foe.

The two fought onwards, driving the orcs back, when a body crashed down in front of their feet. It was a mangled elf and they looked up to see a giant cave ogre wading into the elven line. The captains pushed and shoved themselves toward the behemoth that was twice as tall as the elves.

The ogre, wearing long chainmail obviously made from many sets sewn together, came just in their reach and they both dispensed with the orcs in front of them. The giant iron-spiked head of a mace swished within inches of the two warriors. The ogre reversed its swing and brought the mace over his head and back down, crushing an elf to the floor.

Both captains stepped forward, their swords ringing against the armor of the ogre, and the monster brought its mace around and slammed it down on the cavern floor. The two elves calmly side-stepped the giant weapon as it sparked when it hit bare stone. Trimimar was then slammed forward by an orc and he bounced off the shaft of the mace. He turned and sliced the arm from the orc that had struck him. The orc's blow had sent him stumbling in between the mace and the ogre and his shoulder now pained him.

Using his keen eyesight, the elf picked out a small hole in the stitched together chain mail and with all his might he drove his sword through the opening deep into the creature's body. The ogre howled in pain and grasped the wound. Arantir sprang straight up in the air, swinging his sword over-hand and bringing it right down on the bony wrist of the ogre trying to hold on to the mace's handle. The elven-made blade struck true and cleanly severed the evil beast's wrist. The mace was left standing in the middle of the battle field with the ogre's hand still dangling from a stout rawhide rope used to keep the weapon from flying away from him during combat.

The two elves stood panting. The ogre tucked his right arm under the pit of his left arm, turned and ran through and over all the orcs that crowded behind him.

The two friends only had a second to nod to each other before the tide of orcs advanced to fill in the void left by the wounded ogre. Then it was back to hacking and slashing as their soldiers shored up the line.

All around them the elves of light fought the dark elves or Illanni and the orcs. Beings that had been meant to live millennia now died in the darkness of the underworld. Then general Orthorion saw the orcs break, their will to fight wrung out of them by the ferocious defense of the elves and by the charge of the two captains of the rear guard.

Only the Illanni and their commanders, the vampires, were left. They refused to leave the field of battle and fought on to the last dark elf. Slowly, one by one, the vampires were picked off by the elves whose concentrated attacks led to their downfall. When the vampires' numbers waned, the Illanni began to break.

First one, then two Illanni flitted out through one of the tunnels, and soon the army broke en-masse and raced for the tunnel's safety.

CHAPTER TWENTY

In the depths of the Illanni underworld the company waited for a messenger from the city, but once he arrived, his appearance put the company ill at ease. The dark elf was whip cord thin with greasy hair and a pocked marked face and he looked to have had a rough life. They judged him a turncoat, if ever one looked like it. He was told who the message was for, but he never showed any emotion. He just took the message and the pouch of gold he was given by Theiors and without a word set off down the passage at a run.

Theiors watched him go.

"Taurnil's not much to look at," he said, "but he moves in and out of the city with ease. He knows every nook and cranny. He also, knows all the right Illanni that live in the low places where the vampires seldom venture. Too many have died in the slums, and they only go to that area in large groups and even then, only with great caution."

"Good," Morganna said. "Now we need to set up the meeting place."

The rebels and Morganna's friends scouted out the environs of her old rooms and picked the places where they would leave guards. At each point Theiors instructed the rebel Illanni to let Boltrein through, but they should sound the alarm should any others accompany him or if there were others that might follow. They were not to fight, but to escape as best they could and make their way to the new area where the rebels were operating from.

Morganna and Theiors descended a level deeper and led the others down into a funnel like cave system where the resistance could ambush the followers.

•　　•　　•　　•　　•

The dark elf messenger Taurnil dodged in and out of the network of passages as he made his way to the slums of the city. He had been born and raised there and he knew every turn like the back of his hand. He had been cast out of society when his family had been destroyed after some now forgotten dispute, but if it had not been for a nurse maid spiriting him away, he would have died along with the rest of the family.

His mission was simple, and he could have pulled it off himself had the vampires not taken control of Illan. They had patrols all over the city, but they dared not enter the slums for fear of being attacked by its inhabitants, not only the Illanni rebels and refugees, but also the monsters of the underworld that had taken up living in the dangerous slum area. The Illanni seldom went down there without a full company of their finest soldiers.

Taurnil made his way through the narrow streets constantly scanning the area, not for fear of the vampires, but for the other inherent dangers of the area. He did not want to end up the victim of an overzealous band of robbers or some other unearthly beast. One reason he chose to look as ragged as he did was because life in the slums was dangerous. The vampires caused him concern, but the denizens of this area cared even less for life. It was kill or be killed. They usually left families alone, but a single Illanni had better be constantly aware of his surroundings.

Most of the buildings in the slum were made of rough-cut stone and seemed to hang over the street. The darkness there took on a life of its own and the occasional torch fought a losing battle against the dark. Taurnil cut back and forth through the darker sections of the street, his Illanni eyes allowing him to see in the near blackness.

He was headed to a tavern on the border of the slums where he hoped to meet a trader that plied his trade from the black-market goods of the slums to the houses of the Illanni elite. He was off limits to the Illanni vampires because more often than not he obtained better food provisions than the Illanni caravans themselves carried.

Taurnil suddenly felt that he was being watched and from the depths of one darkened alley came a voice.

"Well, my old friend, what do you carry this time?"

The dark elf messenger drew a dagger with his left hand and he slowed to a stop. He was aware there were several shadows in the darkness surrounding him, but he did not wait for further dialogue. He drew his sword and with his dagger still in his other hand he ran at the figure to his left.

The ambusher that had been in front of him advanced and Taurnil attacked. He neatly skewered that one after a flurry of sword strokes. Immediately Taurnil did a summersault and landed right in front of his last attacker, too close for his adversary's sword to be of any use. Two quick slashes of Taurnil's dagger and his attacker fell. The blood had not stopped squirting from the creature's neck before Taurnil took off running.

He more sensed then saw that something had been thrown at his fleeing form, and he tucked down into a shoulder roll as an object flew right over him. If he had been standing, he would have been pierced by the spear that had been thrown by another assailant.

●　　　●　　　●　　　●　　　●

Taurnil reached the tavern without any further problems. It was a stout building and offered the appearance of the upper level of the city, where many buildings were often set aside by themselves as was this one. The stone was still rough cut, but the three-story building had mortar holding the stones together like the more expensive houses in other parts of the city.

He ducked into the building and scanned the crowded tap room. In the corner sat his man, Talskorn the trader, and Taurnil slid through the crowd and was soon at his table. The trader was a huge half orc with a big barrel chest and a gut to match. His face bore resemblance to his human ancestry, but his body was hairy beyond belief.

Talskorn stood and slapped the messenger a hearty blow on the back which sent him forward and bumping into another tabletop.

"What does my little friend need this time?" asked the hairy half orc.

Taurnil righted himself and replied in a hushed voice.

"I need this to be delivered to Boltrein, Lord Tibersu's son."

The half orc's face turned serious.

"You know what kind of trouble I can get into if this is found out. I'll be strung up by my ankles and bled to death for those heathen vampires to drink."

"I know it's dangerous," replied the Illanni, "but you will be well paid for this delivery."

"Well paid should be a lot, considering the danger," Talskorn opined. "I expect three times my usual payment."

The Illanni had been prepared and he had a pouch with five times the gold the half orc usually charged. Deftly he counted out the gold under the table and handed over three times the usual payment to the trader. He would pocket the rest.

The half orc hefted the weight in his big hairy hand. Through his years of trading he knew that the messenger had given him the right amount of gold and not some counterfeited coin. Besides, he thought, if the dark elf Taurnil did cheat the trader, his life would be over. Every bounty hunter in the warrens would be after him.

He smiled at the Illanni and received the wrapped message that was passed discreetly under the table. At that Taurnil rose and without a word lost himself in the crowd.

Taurnil whispered as he faded into the crowd.

"May the gods go with you, my friend."

• • • • •

The half orc gathered his belongings and met the rest of his hirelings in the stables of the tavern. It was a motley group of seven orcs and two Illanni guards. Talskorn motioned to them to get the mules and they preceded cautiously into the upper city.

Before reaching Tibersu's estate, he called on several houses where he traded gold for fresh vegetables only several days from the surface. When he reached the Tibersu Estate he went into the kitchen where the cook was busy looking over the half orc's goods. Talskorn beckoned to a small dark elf, a servant or more likely a slave. Flipping him a gold piece,

Talskorn handed over the message and gave instructions to hand it to Lord Boltrein and him alone.

CHAPTER TWENTY-ONE

Boltrein was standing alone on one of the balconies of his family home and staring across the cityscape of Illan. It was dark, what the above grounders would call twilight, but it was the norm there ever since the cursed Taza had taken control and then his father had gained control of the city.

The need for blood was intense as he had not fed in several days. Being a vampire had its advantages—he was stronger and quicker—but the continual need for blood outweighed them. Did the means outweigh the gains?

He hated the thought of arrogantly choosing and feeding on a slave, or on one of his own kind, and for him, in this situation, it was unclear whether the fuzziness of instinct versus any heightened consciousness now clouded his judgment. His last feeding had been on a horse, but that had only slated his thirst for a while.

Oh, the hunger, it drove him, he knew, but his every waking thought was concerned with it. A curse, he had recently called it, and he now knew being a vampire was a curse. Turned away by his father, not by his own volition, his life now gave him odd thoughts. He could see that his father's thinking was right for the Illanni. Boltrein understood that if they were to forever band together and survive the hardships of the underworld, then being a vampire helped.

In fact, he himself had been able to imagine this noble quest furthering their cause for survival and for saving his dark elf race before the trials of the underworld claimed them all.

He slammed his fist on the rail of the balustrade and the stone crumbled and fell into the courtyard. Yes, he thought, his was a new found strength, but the cost of it was that so many of his people had been killed when newly turned vampires went on their killing sprees. The power of being a vampire was all consuming and it quickly took control of all the faculties of the turned.

His turning had been forced upon him, but luckily his sister had escaped. Now he knew that she aided the Illanni rebels to find freedom above ground. On one side it went against what being an Illanni meant. On the other, he was happy for his sister, but his happiness soured when he realized the potential she was robbing from her people. They already had enough trouble battling the creatures that stalked the under dark without her weakening the ability of her race to do that.

Now, married to a surface elf, Morganna was gone from his life, just like his mother. He slapped his forehead. He had all these problems and situations, but no sure answers.

A light knock on the door startled him from his train of thought and he called out, "Enter."

A small, young Illanni slave opened the door and came into the room and Boltrein could smell the fear on this one. How he had escaped being fed upon was a mystery to him, Boltrein knew. Usually such menial stock had already been used as food. By the gods, Boltrein thought, how can I even contemplate such horror?

The small Illanni dark one walked meekly across the room with the bound message in his hand. The slave held out the missive and Boltrein snatched the paper away, snarling at the child. It quickly turned and escaped out the door.

Boltrein was displeased with himself about how he had responded, to the slave, but it had come naturally. The need for feeding was strong within him and he could hardly contain it. Boltrein unfolded the message and stared at it for several clicks of the clock. There was no mistaking his sister's handwriting. He read the contents.

My dear brother,

I am in need of your assistance. Can you come to my old room where I hid from father? If so, I will be there tomorrow.

Morganna

She was here near the city, Boltrein thought. Instantly the idea of capturing her swirled through his mind. His father would look on him proudly if he could capture Morganna, the rebel. But no. He shook his head to clear his thoughts. This was his sister, his blood, and that transcended his father's wishes.

His thoughts turned again to blood and to his ever-growing hunger. He forced it out of his mind.

Whatever Morganna needed, it had to be important for her to reach out to him. She could never be sure of his reaction. No one could be sure of any vampire's reaction. This was a mystery that even he had to learn the secrets to.

He would have to chance the meeting and just control his blood thirst.

He crossed to a table where a thick stub of a candle was burning and set the message aflame and then crumbled the ashes in his hand before leaving the room.

The blood thirst called. He headed to the stables.

The next morning Boltrein left his room fully armored and made his way down the stairs to the courtyard. Everybody that he passed bowed and Boltrein could feel the sheer terror of him that their bodies exuded. After one final, quick and soothing stop at the stables, he was ready to find his sister. The guards at the gate snapped to attention as he passed, and he soon disappeared into the darkness.

Once clear of the gates and eyes of the vigilant guards, he slipped the hood of his cape up and veered his path towards the slums. The slums were dangerous to lone Illanni dark ones and to vampires alike, but he knew that it was the best way to lose any followers that might be on his trail.

CHAPTER TWENTY-TWO

Boltrein had never been in the slums before, but to escape any patrols or single vampires he knew he had to go through that section of the city. He wasn't sure exactly which streets to take, but he headed west and hoped that direction would take him where he wanted to go.

Once he had traveled deep into the shadowy slums, Boltrein turned one narrow corner and collided with a dark figure that immediately threw back its hood to reveal no face. The pain Boltrein experienced was terrific and his mind felt like it was exploding.

He had just bumped into a Juc, a lesser demon that attacked using its mental acuity. The assault had been so sudden that Boltrein stumbled to his knees and he grabbed his head with his hands. In his mind he heard the Juc laughing.

The Illanni vampire had never experienced such pain. He felt like his head was slowly cooking and about to explode. He could feel blood from his nose and the corners of his eyes dribbling down his face. His hearing was gone too. Struggling against the pain, he shakily sought his sword handle and with his whole body beginning to convulse, he weakly drew it from its sheath. The Juc was now standing above him and it continued its mental attack.

Boltrein's sword flew in a wild arc and sliced across the thighs of the demon. The Juc let go of the vampire Boltrein's mind, but the Illanni could hear the painful scream from the demon echoing in his head. Boltrein had just gotten to his knees, but the piercing scream knocked him into a fetal position.

The outburst of the Juc's pain gave Boltrein a moment's relief, though, and gave him enough time to get back up on his knees. He struck again and by this time he had regained some of his faculties and he could thrust harder with his sword.

He aimed right where the Juc's heart should be, but the attack did nothing except bring more pain to the Juc. Boltrein's head rang with the Juc's mental scream and Boltrein dropped to the ground again. He managed to pull his sword free and he struck at the creature's head. The Juc dodged the blow, but the sword sheared off a portion of the Juc's muscled shoulder.

The demon attacked again. Boltrein's mind erupted and pain shot down the length of his body. Only his vampiric strength enabled him to hold on to the sword without giving into the pain or the threat of eventual death. He struck at the Juc again. From his kneeling position, his sword's arc connected with the demon's knee. It cut through sinew and tendons, but his swing was still too weak to sever the leg completely.

Again the creature cried in agony and this time it toppled over on its side. Boltrein saw he had his chance and he struck at the creature again. There was more force behind his blow as he aimed at the Juc's head and the edge of the sword cleaved so deep into the demon that Boltrein heard it scrape against the stone road beneath the demon's head.

This time there was no scream of pain to echo inside Boltrein's head. The creature was dead beside him.

Leaning on his sword, Boltrein the vampire stood with difficulty. He was confused and the blood coming from his eyes momentarily blinded him. Propping himself up against a building, he wiped the blood away from his face and found that his ears had been damaged as well and his hearing was limited. His ears were caked with blood. He cleaned them off and he could hear a little better.

Boltrein lurched down the street away from the dead Juc. It would be just his luck, he thought, for the thing to be traveling in a pair. But if it had been, he realized, he would not have survived.

●   ●   ●   ●

After a full turn of the clock wandering through the maze of the slums, Boltrein came to the edge of the city without any further difficulties. By now he had regained his faculties and was feeling his old self again. He knew that the strength of his being a vampire was all that had saved him from the demon and then let him restore himself so quickly.

The uneven stone streets gave way to the smooth cavern floor and he quickly made his way into one of the many tunnels that emptied out around the city. Again, he took a circuitous route, climbing ever higher through the stone tunnels.

As he neared his sister's old rooms, he passed a rebel guard post and he could hear the beating of several hearts hidden in a side room. He admired the caution that Morganna was taking and assumed that there were similar watchers surrounding the whole area. The rebel underground was taking precaution that he might be leading an Illanni attack force.

He knew seeing his younger sister would bring back a flood of memories, both good and bad. The worst would be remembering her escape from his father's clutches that fateful day. Only now could he see the inevitable means that his father had been taking. The only way to ensure their race's future was through the population all becoming powerful vampires. The other elves of light had forsaken them. Where else could they turn but to vampirism in this underground warren of monsters and hazards?

Thousands had died before Taza had shown them that lighted path. Certainly, Taza had turned out to be a fraud, but he had planted the seed to their salvation. Boltrein truly believed this.

Now his sister had called out to him. She had been his closest friend and confidante before Taza had arrived. She had herself escaped being turned and now she led the rebels. He found it most repulsive that she had married a wood elf, though, as they were one of the clans that had forsaken their brothers to die in the underworld.

He recognized he was near the doorway to her old rooms. What was this going to be like...he the predator meeting with his kind's prey? He slowly pushed on the door. She had been true to her word. He could only hear the one heart beating.

He opened the door, and she stood before him, alone. She was dressed for the underworld in thick, tough pants and a leather jacket with iron scales sewn on. Her auburn hair looked different somehow from when he had last known her.

He wondered what other differences in her there could be from living above ground?

CHAPTER TWENTY-THREE

Martish's dark elf soldiers fired volley after volley toward their enemies and then the vampire in charge of her section called on them all to march toward the elves. Martish fought for her soldiers, not for some vampire. She knew she was in charge of her own free will.

Soon all she saw in front of her was an interlocked wall of shields as the elves of light marched forward. She reached the wall, clashing into it, and those across from her strained to keep their wall intact. Her long sword reached across it and pierced an elf's eye. He fell and Martish kicked another elf now trying to recover the integrity of the wall.

She was pushed forward by the rest of her company which followed her as the attackers and defenders mingled into one of mass of confusion. Her sword as light as a feather, Martish began swinging left and right to keep two elves at bay. Her magical sword began to take over the fight, darting this way and that, and killing or wounding an elf of light with every stroke.

She waded deeper into the elven reserves with the help of her magical sword, but her second in command grabbed her shoulder almost prying it off with his strength.

"Our company has lost too many soldiers. We need to retreat," the dark elf yelled.

Martish scanned the area and saw that too many of her soldiers were down. It took only a single click of the clock for her to make up her mind.

"Sound the retreat!" she shouted.

The company began falling back, their shields held high, as the elves drove them from the field of battle with a massive barrage of arrows.

The vampire in charge of her section of attack appeared and began swinging his sword at the retreating Illanni. When he saw Martish, the vampire strode though the hail of arrows towards her.

"Why have you disobeyed me?" the dark elf vampire asked her.

Martish felt the pain in her right shoulder before she could answer the elven arrow that had just pierced her body.

The vampire smiled at her.

"Easy prey," it said and, raising its sword, it struck downward with all its unnatural strength.

Martish knew she was about to die and she shifted her sword to her left hand. Two of her company jumped on the back of the vampire, but it threw them off with ease.

Its sword struck down and crashed against Martish's blade. A fiery blast ensued and the vampire's sword broke in two. She recovered from the blast and struck past the dark one's guard and impaled her sword into its abdomen.

There was a single click of the clock in which Martish thought she saw confusion on the monster's face, but then it disintegrated before her eyes. As she stared at the ash pile that had been the vampire, two of her soldiers pulled her upright and dragged her back into a tunnel.

The sword the dragon had given her had finally revealed its true nature in this free for all melee. The dragon had known what she would face and had chosen the sword accordingly.

The two soldiers held their shields high above Martish to keep the elven arrows at bay until they had finally pulled her through the opening of the passage that the whole company knew had to be a tunnel to the surface. They propped Martish against the wall and one of her company took out the arrow. Another dark elf had gotten a vial ready from his backpack and he tipped it up so Martish could drink it.

Almost immediately the warm draught spread through her body and healed the damage she had suffered. The healer tightly bound her shoulder and only then she allowed Martish a chance to stand.

She stood up, arm in a sling, her shoulder still stinging from the wound, and surveyed the aftermath of the battle. Already the other Illanni were retreating, but a handful came to the passage Martish and her company were hiding in.

These were quickly pushed ahead of the remaining dark elves of her company. Little did they know they had just signed up to be in Martish's raiders. Several orcs also tried to gain the relative safety of the cave, but they were cut down.

"This tunnel leads to the surface," Martish told her followers, "and I can't think of a better place to be at the moment. Move out and explain to the new soldiers that they have just volunteered to be our comrades."

She was saddened to see that her company now numbered only a third of what their strength had been before she had been enlisted by Tibersu. Martish did not care that they had died, though. She was more concerned about the course ahead for them once out in the Mordolwyn mountains.

Her company of Illanni had just begun to march upward when several of the new enlistees voiced concerns about their situation. Martish made her way up from the back of the column and saw two new Illanni with their hands bound tightly behind their backs. Martish looked at these two and then gestured to the twelve other new dark elf soldiers gathered together around them.

"Ride with me or die," she told them simply.

With her sword she then ran both bound dissenters through. The new soldiers all stood straighter.

"Yes, captain!" was all they said.

●   ●   ●   ●   ●

"It has been some time," Morganna said warily to her brother.

"Yes, it has," Boltrein responded in a distance voice.

They both examined each other and tried to choose carefully what would happen in the next few moments.

Morganna broke their unease by saying, "I am glad you have come."

"Well," he said, "I almost didn't make it. I encountered a Juc in the slums and had quite the time of it." He showed her the traces of blood trailing down his face.

"I'm glad you're alright," she said. "Are you alone?"

"Of course. I'm your brother still and would not lie to my own sister."

She smiled at him.

"You're also a vampire, and that leaves a lot to be desired as far as trust goes."

"Yes, but your message does have me intrigued."

She went up to him and gave him a hug.

"It is so nice to see you. Really," she said.

He hugged her back and could hear Morganna's heart and feel her blood pumping through her system.

When they let go of each other, Morganna was smiling the old smile that Boltrein had come to love. The vampire knew he could never harm his sister or allow her to be harmed. He loved her too much.

"I need your help," Morganna told him.

He nodded, but asked warily, "And that help would be what exactly?"

His sister weighed her next comment.

"I need you to help me get to father."

Boltrein laughed. It was his habit of late since he had been turned.

"That's easy enough. I tie you up and take the prize to him. There. It's just that easy."

She was shaking her head at him but smiling.

"You still have your wit about you, brother."

He shrugged good naturedly.

"I have to cling on to my mortality some way," he said. "Now, why would you want to see father. He'll surely kill you at first sight."

"Simple. We mean to depose him," Morganna said.

Her vampire brother laughed again.

"You mean you intend to kill him. The elves of light have advanced and now you show up in Illan. It doesn't take a sage to come up with that conclusion."

"You know what he is doing is wrong. Our people hide in fear and escape the city to be rescued. It is not the natural course of things."

"But why kill the one Illanni trying to save our race?" her brother answered back. "Vampirism is a means to an end. And that end is to save our people, our race."

"No, that end is to enslave our people," she argued back.

"No, you're wrong, sister. Only those who are willing to be turned are turned. No one is turned against their will."

"That is an outright lie that father has told you," she countered. "I have had too many escaped Illanni tell me of families being dragged from their homes and turned into vampires in Taza's temple. This has to end."

"What do you propose, little sister?" he asked. He was beginning to grow tired of the give and take and he was feeling the hunger for blood coming to him.

She studied his face, trying to judge if he was on her side or her father's.

"I just need to get a company of mine into the temple. We will take it from there."

He sighed and took a deep pull from his flask, filled with horse blood.

"It just can't be done," he said. "The guards would smell you out. They would hear your blood coursing through your veins."

"Well, how can it be done then?" she asked.

He looked hard at the floor while he thought. After two clicks of the clock he spoke.

"I will have to take you all the way to father. I can get you by the guards and into the inner sanctum, but I can't promise everything will go according to plan."

Morganna looked deep into his eyes.

"Would you do that for me?"

Boltrein looked around the empty room.

"What you propose will be the end of our capital Illan as we know it. Only father holds the city in check through his firm hand. It will be chaos and the elven army will be able to walk right in and kill us all."

"No," she said. "The army will fall back once the threat is overcome. Father is that threat."

"All that I know will be gone," he said quietly. "I will have to run and hide, doomed to forever to be a denizen of the underworld."

"That's not true" she said. "You can come with me and we'll find somewhere for you."

He looked deep into her eyes.

"No, I'll forever be a pariah. Hated and hunted. Forever on the run. If I do this for you, I am condemning myself to eventual death."

"You must do this for our people. We must stay together as a race. Father is pulling us apart and it must end."

Boltrein closed his eyes and nodded.

"Your argument is sound. For the fate of our race I will lead you into the temple and to father."

Boltrein waited while Morganna called for her friends.

Soon the other members of her company entered the room. Botreg and Hority stood by the door the latter's odor was too much for the enclosed area. Morganna made the introductions, but the high elf barely nodded. She introduced Eldahir as her husband and Boltrein smiled.

"So, the rumors were true. I somewhat hesitantly welcome you into our family. I hope you like vampires because the majority of us are."

Eldahir replied diplomatically. "I am a very tolerant elf."

"Good," Boltrein said, "because, like it or not, your lives will be in my hands once we enter the city."

"How do you plan to get us into the city…and eventually into the temple?" asked Celedant.

"Ah, wizard," Boltrein said, "that is a good question. I intend to take you through the slums and up to the city proper, but it will not be an easy stroll. I was nearly killed myself in the slums while making my way here."

"Then shouldn't we take another route?" Tarquin asked,

Boltrein shook his head no.

"I was attacked by accident and only being alone was I a good target in the slums. Our group is large enough to keep us safe. At least that is what I am planning on, unless our dragon friends decide to morph back into their original forms."

"You mean you can tell us apart from the rest?" Azimuth asked,

Boltrein laughed, something he had been doing a lot lately.

"I can hear all of your hearts beating and yours are different. Plus, your blood smells of dragon kind."

The two dragons bowed and Azimuth said, "I am little trained in the ways of vampirism, but I find it an astonishing feat you have just proved."

The high elf spoke sternly to all in the room.

"We need to forget these frivolities," she said, "and get on with the mission."

Boltrein gave her an icy stare.

"Of course, my lady. We do waste time. But I must gauge my new allies before I lead them out into the city." He pointed to Ress, "I sense great loss and a hidden hatred within you, little one."

Tarquin put a protective arm around his new wife, but she chose to speak.

"I despise firedrakes," she said. "They destroyed my village and they," she motioned to the others in the room, "they found me and gave me something worthwhile to fight."

"I did not mean to offend, you," Boltrein said, "The man beside you must be Tarquin, the hero of Brackus, and the destroyer of Taza. I cannot thank you enough for that act."

Tarquin offered his hand and Boltrein took it.

"Well met, Boltrein," Tarquin said.

Celedant asked, "Might I enquire as to why you would turn your back to your kind?"

Boltrein gave him an evil smile.

"'My kind' you are right to say. But not all who are turned are willing subjects. I realize the advantages this gives the dark elf race in the underworld, but unlike the majority, for me to live this way is repulsive in a way you might never understand. My sister has helped me see the true path for my people...one of light, instead of darkness."

The wizard nodded at Boltrein.

"A noble cause, I might add. I have a feeling we are in good hands."

The dragon Elanesse added, "Though I sense great evil in the other vampires that I have encountered, I sense that you speak the truth and act for your people, and not for evil."

"Come," said Boltrein. "We must go. There is no night or day here in the underworld, but our time is still precious if we plan to beat the battle that is about to come."

Morganna's rebels lined the passage as Boltrein led the company out of the room. To see a vampire and not be afraid of it or not attack it was something new to the Illanni freedom fighters. What they thought was the cause of all their oppression and troubles was now walking among them without a moment's hesitation.

As they made their way through the tunnels and passages, the dark elf vampire called back to them all.

"This passage opens near the slums and if I was followed, it is there that I would expect an attack. So, we must be very cautious in that area. Once in the slums we're as safe as safe can be. The Illanni seldom venture into that portion of the city, but there are many dangers lurking in the dark. I would not use magic. It might summon guards."

They quickly made their way to the opening of the tunnel and Boltrein motioned for them to stay behind. In the semi darkness of the city they could see that a mere fifty paces separated them from the first of the ramshackle buildings that began the slums of Illan.

Boltrein ventured out in front of them and scanned everywhere for anything suspicious. He stood tall and haughty, like a vampire would, almost seeming to invite an attack. After he was sure that they would not be attacked, he motioned for all the others to follow.

They entered the slums and the smell of rotten food, and worse, greeted their nostrils. Hority sprang for the garbage with a religious furor in his eyes and Botreg had to grab him around the waist and turn him back towards the company.

Botreg scolded him.

"We must finish the mission first. Then I'll be happy to accompany you back into this warren."

"This is indeed a holy place," the smelly dwarf replied. "I sense Clor's work here. There will be much to catalog in these streets and alleys."

They were a block into the slums when from out of the buildings round them screamed an assortment of attackers. They were only base robbers, but they were numerous, and they ran the gamut of all the underworld's denizens.

The company formed a circle as best they could and defended themselves. Celedant wielded his staff and crushed various skulls and bones. Tarquin and Eldahir plied their swords on the mixture of attackers and cut them down as they engaged the two warriors. Half orcs, orcs and displaced dark elf Illanni all swarmed over the group. Ress spun and thrust her spear it into her attackers and pushed them off with quick kicks to their bodies.

Inwe used a delicate, but hardened sword to clear the attackers in front of her. Her sword would bend like it was about to break, but she quickly gained the upper hand and lunged with astonishing accuracy into her opponents. The two dragons, still in elven form, bounded into the mass of attackers and dealt death to them with their swords. They barely noticed the feeble attacks by the robbers.

Meanwhile Boltrein had spun around and waded into the largest mass of attackers, unconcerned about the superficial wounds that he received. His vampire body healed the small wounds as fast as it was injured. Hority danced around his attackers dealing quick death with his magical branch. He would strike one robber and then bound away and roll into a tight new stance only to strike out at the next robber's feet. Botreg stayed to the side and protected Tarquin's back.

The smartest of the robbers quickly realized what they were up against, but the most inexperienced attacked the company and soon their bodies began piling up. Soon all the attackers withdrew back into the shadows.

"They're a simple band of robbers," Boltrein explained. "Their numbers have been substantial here in the slums, but they stay here and don't bother the city. Hence, they are allowed to eke out a life. Let's hurry onwards now. We must be away from here lest we attract unwanted attention. Those who prey on carrion will be here soon."

CHAPTER TWENTY-FOUR

Orthorion sent his soldiers leaping forward and hounding the retreating Illanni.

The vampires stayed and fought to the last and left many dead elves heaped around them before the blood thirsty creatures themselves could be overwhelmed and killed. The elves of light harried the rear of the Illanni and there was no mercy asked nor given. Their arrows flew after the retreating Illanni and elven foot soldiers charged into the rear of the fleeing dark elf army and cut the stragglers down.

Orthorion knew this might be the deciding victory in the war and he pressed his attack home.

The elves cut down the Illanni and captured whole groups of prisoners. Soon it became a logistical nightmare to both continue the attack and control the prisoners, and General Orthorion ordered his troops to cease fighting.

The elves of light were hard to restrain, though, from chasing the retreating Illanni, their mortal enemies, into the tunnels. They had seen their friends wounded or killed at the hands of the Illanni and the blood lust they usually were able to contain had now risen within them.

•   •   •   •   •

The Illanni had suffered most of the casualties and many vampires had been killed while many more dark elves captured. Even the vampires that lived had been vaporized by magical spells from the high elves' wizards and sorceresses. As much as the elves despised the act of killing prisoners, vampires were a special case and were seen as the ultimate evil that had held the Illanni under their sway.

The Illanni prisoners were open to being given the choice of staying alive and they would not fight their captors any longer. Some even volunteered to go ahead of the army and try to talk the other dark elves they encountered into surrendering.

The elves ruled that too hazardous, though, because the Illanni prisoners had seen too much of the attacking army and they could not be trusted. Instead, they were sent under heavy escort back the way the army had come and were led up towards the surface.

The dead elves of light were laid to the side of the cavern and cairns were built over them while the enemies' dead were merely piled in an off-shoot tunnel.

While the dead and wounded were being taken care of behind the army's lines, General Orthorion noted that most of the enemy had fled down the middle passage and had left behind many Illanni and orc corpses that had been cut down by the attacking elves at the mouth of the passage. He called for the captains of the rear guard, Trimimar and Arantir.

They finally came up to the general after a quarter turn of the clock and Orthorion welcomed them.

"I am glad to see the two of you survived the battle," he told them. "It was a close-run thing. Until the vampires started falling, the battle could have gone either way."

Both soldiers agreed and the general continued.

"I need you to take your soldiers and follow the Illanni. See where that tunnel leads."

They nodded their heads at the command and went off to collect the remainder of their company.

• • • •

Their company behind them, the two captains cautiously advanced up the tunnel and found many wounded or dead enemies as they went. At several points Illanni stood unarmed in front of them and were willing to surrender rather than go back under the control of the vampires.

When they met any remaining vampires, the Illanni fought them and continued battling the company of elves to a standstill until the evil commanders could be killed.

The two captains left the enemy wounded and prisoners for the advancing army to handle.

•   •   •   •   •

Boltrein led the company east through the maze of the slums, turning left and right at random, until he thought them safe from anyone following. They walked by rough stone buildings that passed for houses or small businesses, but were in a dreadful state of disrepair. The families of orcs and some low born Illanni had scraped out a living there, but now they barely looked at the company as they walked by. They knew that a vampire was at the head of the column.

Boltrein was leading them a leisurely pace so he could remain ever watchful. The company kept hoods of their cloaks up and all the while the vampire kept heading towards the city proper. They caught fleeting glimpses of towering villas, their great stone columns holding up the roofs, their facades carved into individual clan fortresses by the Illanni. Tarquin knew that the elves had no chance to besiege the city, let alone take it.

Finally, Boltrein slowed them down.

"Take care. We are near to the road that leads up into the city."

They turned off the road that they had been following and the Illanni went in to search a house and the company took shelter in a rundown, two-story home. They shut the door behind them and Boltrein disappeared up the stairs.

He was back down in several clicks of the clock.

"I stopped here to see if we are being followed," he said. "We Illanni are good at tracking, stalking…and paranoia. Once we have rested here for some time, we will continue."

There was a great commotion from the direction of the road into the city. The dark elf motioned to his cohorts and said, "Let us see what is happening."

They all went up the stairs to a small room which had a window that looked out at the road. In between the houses they could see a large host of Illanni and their allies marching back to the city.

"They're the soldiers sent to battle the elves," Boltrein said.

"They do not look like they won," Celedant observed.

"Look at that wagon," Tarquin said and pointed to a wagon being pulled by orcs. It was full of wounded dark elves. Another wagon and then another and then another followed the first.

"They had to have been beaten," Tarquin said, "and are retreating or their healers would have had time to see to the wounded."

"Come!" Boltrein said. "This is a perfect time to enter the city. There will be mass confusion and we can slip into the temple. You need to tap into your body's reserve strength now. There is not a single click of the clock to lose."

There were moans from several of the members, but they all started moving nevertheless.

They entered back into the downstairs portion of the house and saw there was a swirling red and yellow vortex forming in front of the door.

"Beware!" Boltrein called out. "Something has followed us and seeks to destroy our company."

Three figures stepped out from the swirling mist.

"Jucs!" Boltrein shouted.

One wore the robes of nobility a swirling pattern of purple and black. Its two companions were less decorated. Suddenly in each of the minds of Boltrein's company was heard the leader of the Jucs.

"Little elf, did you think you could get away with killing one of my children? I think not," they each felt pain shoot through their minds as they all collapsed to the floor.

Ress gathered what strength she had as she fell and threw her spear. It slammed into one of the younger Jucs and pinned him to the door. Not only did the Jucs' mental acuity ring painfully through the company's heads, but now the screams of the injured one did too.

Azimuth and Elanesse, both dragons and immune to the Jucs' attacks, jumped the railing of the stairs and landed in front of the demons. The dragon high elf quickly dispatched the wounded Juc thrusting its sword through the demon's chest and then turned to the master. The Juc facing Azimuth pulled out a wicked looking, mace that dripped a black substance. The dragon could only guess it was poison. Its mace swung out at Azimuth and even though he blocked it, the black matter sprayed across Azimuth burning his skin and slowly eating through his clothing.

Meanwhile, on the stairs Celedant was fighting the Jucs' mental attack by pulling on all his years of training on Dragon Isle. Suddenly the invading mental attack eased in his mind and then it ended. He had quickly cast a strong silencing spell intended to stop the Juc's telepathy as well as any other sound around him.

He cleared his eyes and looked around him and saw the others slowly falling into sitting positions, but still using the railing to try to keep standing.

Elanesse held her long slender blade as she attacked the Juc master, but it used its bare arms to block her blows. To the dragon it was like chopping a granite rock and all the time she was swinging, the master Juc laughed.

Azimuth then pieced the younger Juc's defense by stabbing it deeply in the stomach. As the monster tried to pull the sword out, Azimuth, with his amazing dragon strength, kicked the creature against the far wall. The Juc bounced back and fell at Azimuth's feet and the dragon stabbed downwards and severed the spine as well as pinned the creature to the floor. Azimuth pulled his sword out of the floor and stabbed the beast in the back of its skull.

Azimuth turned and saw the sparks flying as the Juc master fended off Elanesse's sword with its bare arms. Azimuth stepped behind the creature and again using his draconic strength he stabbed the demon in the back, where its heart should have been. He felt a tremendous resistance to his sword, but finally the point of it began to penetrate the beast's natural armor. Azimuth's arm gained momentum and the point of his sword ballooned out the front of the demon's robe spewing yellow blood.

The Juc master pivoted and with a quick shove sent Azimuth crashing out the door and flying out into the street. This gave Elanesse time and she thrust her blade at the creature as it turned to engage her again. The tip of her blade slid into the Juc's neck and with one quick, strong movement her sword ripped out the demon's throat. Blood spewed upwards and the creature fell dying to the floor.

It took a number of clicks of the clock for all the others to recover from the mental attack, and the two dragons stood watch at the door while the company gathered their wits back about themselves.

Boltrein went up and consulted with the dragons.

"Do you hear anything," he asked. "or have you seen anyone looking suspicious about the street?"

Azimuth said, "Not a thing has stirred on the streets and I hear nothing out of the ordinary."

The vampire nodded and then called out to the others.

"Come! We must hurry."

CHAPTER TWENTY-FIVE

The passage to the surface ran for miles through the underworld, and the remainder of Martish's dark elvan troops stooped, crawled and slid sideways to escape the vampires until the passage finally came to its end high up on a mountain side.

Her company had brought little in the way of protective clothing, only the leather armor each wore, and she worried how the sun would affect her troops. Stooping on the grass that grew in the desolate place above ground, she dug into the gritty soil. She poured her canteen of water into the exposed dirt and started churning the soil.

She began plastering the mud to her exposed skin and the rest followed suit. Once they were ready, Martish led them down the path while she pondered where they might get fabric, cloaks, or horses.

The ones who suffered the most were the new additions to the company. They had never been above ground. The sun blinded them, and the other members of the company had to lead them down the path by grasping their shoulders.

After a day on the trail, Martish's company came to a dwarvan homestead. She counted ten of the mountain horses in a paddock that dwarves preferred to ride. One dwarf came out of the barn with a bale of hay balanced on his shoulders. Martish motioned toward the house to five of her raiders while she took the dwarf from behind with her dagger. He never saw his death coming.

The five Illanni had dashed off in the direction of the house and they returned as Martish was mounting a regular sized horse she had found in the barn.

She spun her horse around and asked, "The house?"

"A small family. Nothing to bother us," one of her company replied, "We got a good bit of food and homemade beer. We gathered their bedding also to cover us from the sun."

She was proud of her company.

"Save the food for the coming night," she said. "We will divvy it up then."

She ordered some of the soldiers on foot to parallel the path and pointed to several other of the Illanni.

"Collect whatever wildlife you can find," she told them, "and the bedding, give to the new members of the company."

The company continued west with the setting sun in their eyes and Martish pondered what they should do now that they were exiled from Illan. They would be hunted by the wood elves of this mysterious world, but at least she and her soldiers were free of the vampires.

•   •   •   •   •

Boltrein peered up and down the street to make sure the dragons had not missed anything, and they all finally left the small house behind. They angled away from the road into the city and passed by all sorts of creatures drawn to the commotion that the beaten army was making. Boltrein took them up several flights of steps and soon the buildings began to look in better repair.

"We are reaching the area of the city that surrounds the temple complex and the houses of the lords," Boltrein said and motioned them to slow down. "This thick fog is ever present at this level. Some say the lords like it this way so they can feed in privacy."

"Is this how you feed?" Inwe snidely asked.

Boltrein would not let her remarks chide him.

"I feed on our livestock, if truth be told," he said. "Come. We must go."

From out of the shadows a voice asked, "Go where, my friend?"

The dark elf stopped and sidled over towards the sound knowing that a stray vampire had happened to find them.

"We go to my lord Tibersu's house," he said, "if you must know."

The shadowed figure laughed. "Are you taking these blooded beings to feed him. I think not."

Boltrein moved faster than the eye could follow and had his sword out attacking the figure. The clash of their swords was muffled in the dense fog bank that covered them and the dark elf moved gracefully, his sword fairly dancing in the murky air. The two were on equal terms with their swords and the duel continued in earnest as the remaining company surrounded the two fighters watching for more Illanni to come out of the fog at any moment.

The Illanni opponent seemed to be able to take Boltrein's strength in stride and did not give an inch. Their combat did draw some other spectators, but they soon left when they saw the company standing with their weapons drawn.

The two Illanni fought on for a tenth of a turn of the clock, both trying to gain an advantage over the other. Striking out with legs and fists, they fought on, neither giving up nor giving ground. Boltrein was having a hard time vanquishing his opponent and he knew only the strongest of the Illanni would have ventured forth alone into this part of the slums. Boltrein recalled running into the demon earlier and realized there was just no telling what could be lurking around the next corner.

Celedant had had enough. He silently stepped in and with his staff swept the feet out from under the other Illanni. Boltrein was instantly atop the dark one, his knees on the Illanni's chest. Holding the pommel and the back of his sword with his other hand, he began to push the blade against his opponent's throat. Blood started welling up from Boltrein's hand and dripped back down on his adversary.

The enemy's face strained in contortions as he tried to get out from under Boltrein, but its blood slowly came from its mouth and began to trickle down the side of its head. Slowly its struggle subsided and then Boltrein's blade severed its head. It died there in the street, a pile of ash where the body had been.

Boltrein stood atop the ashes, breathing heavily, and Morganna grabbed his sleeve.

"Come! We must hurry," she told him.

Her brother looked at her as if he did not recognize her. He showed his fangs he hissed at her, sounding like sharpening a sword on a grinding stone. His black eyes looked blankly at her and all the while he was smelling her blood and hearing the sound of her heart.

He shook himself to clear his mind and his blood lust subsided his eyes cleared. He looked with sad eyes over at his sister.

"I apologize," he said. "The fight let the vampire part of me take control. I had thought that I had gained my own control back, but obviously not."

She placed a consoling hand on his back. "That will come with time," she said.

"Come now," he said. "We must hurry away from this spot. That fight was sure to have drawn attention to us and a patrol of illanni might appear at any moment."

He led them at a run out of the slums into the more habitable portions of the city.

CHAPTER TWENTY-SIX

After the battle ended, General Orthorion gave his soldiers time to recover from the assault. The elves spread out in the cavern and in the side passages and allowed the healers to work on the wounded. Meanwhile, Orthorion met with the high elf general Rathar Carnesir to discuss their further movements.

They were both in agreement that they should follow the dark Illanni and leave a force of walking wounded to guard the more seriously injured. Once the company was rested and healed as best they could be, the general issued his order for Arantir and Trimimar to resume their positions as rear guards while the rest of the army followed the Illanni.

The elven army quickly started marching to follow the defeated Illanni.

The main force with the rebel Illanni elves leading them, moved quickly through the caves as they followed in the footsteps of their defeated foe. There were no more harassing attacks, just the remnants of the defeated. The dead and the wounded had been left behind as well as weapons and armor that had been thrown off in their desperate attempt to flee the oncoming elves.

Soon the passages opened up into larger galleries with portions of carved stone and in two of them they met some opposition from purely rearguard actions to slow down the elves of light. The vampires had collected enough soldiers willing to fight and still made stands where they could, but the Illanni dark ones and orc soldiers had very little fight left in them and were only being controlled because of their fear of their vampire overlords.

Once the first of the elves of light entered the large cavern, the vampires gathered their followers together and attacked. The first time the elves were driven back into the smaller caves and the fighting was confined to the tunnels.

Many of the vampires' elves fell as the light elves fended off the attacks, and only the vampires held the charges together.

The elves of light could call on reserves while their enemy could not. Soon they were pushing back the Illanni and their vampire overlords. The new fighters spread out in the chamber and attacked in masse while the vampires held the Illanni and orcs together. However, once they saw the Illanni vampires were being killed, many of the dark ones and the orcs retreated or surrendered.

As the army moved on, the dark elves countering their attacks would stand in the smaller tunnels and peppered their opponents with arrows. The Illanni forces would charge the elves of light, but be met by the fresh elven troops and the high elf wizards. Those elves formed a shield wall and the Illanni broke upon it like waves. The veteran, well rested troops that had not been involved in any of the previous fighting would hold the wall and as the engagement turned ferocious, both sides began to engage in close order fighting.

The elves of light's wizards then concentrated on the vampires that stood behind their soldiers chivvied them onwards. Only the fear of their leaders kept the Illanni and orcan soldiers fighting, but soon the vampires themselves could withstand no more of the magical attacks and they charged into the mass of their soldiers to join the fray. Some of the timid vampires ran from the smaller engagements.

The vampires that did attack worked their way through their troops and tore at the shield wall. Using their incredible strength, they broke through the wall, pulling and tossing elves aside in their fury. The fighting here was the worst as the vampires had gone into a fighting frenzy and were difficult to defeat. Many elves fell wounded or dead at their feet.

Soon the elves of light recognized they needed to converge on individual vampires, and they were then able to overwhelm them and kill them, turning them to ash.

When the Illanni dark ones saw there were no more vampires behind them, they dropped their weapons and retreated across the cavern. The remaining Illanni surrendered, except for those most loyal to their lord Tibersu. They fought to the death or until they were overcome by the sheer number of the elves.

These battles occurred three times before the Illanni rebels could lead their main army out upon the plains of Illan. The elves could then slow their advance after all of them had gone through the entrance and mustered before the city.

Boltrein led his company out of the slums with Botreg and Hority as the rear guards. The streets had become less cluttered and wider, but they were still clouded in a dense mist. The company passed several lone illanni going about their business, but none looked at the large group because they didn't want to draw attention to themselves. Lone travelers could easily fall prey to those vampires in the streets out to slate their thirst.

Boltrein stopped at a corner. He motioned them all forward and spoke to the company in a low voice.

"This mist acts as night in this cavern, but it will recede a little once a new cycle begins. So, we must find shelter. Most importantly, if we come across any guards, let me do the talking. Come now. I know where there is an abandoned estate near here."

Boltrein quickened the pace as the mist was dissolving around them and he finally pointed out an estate carved into the curving side of the great cavern. Its empty windows stared out at them like the eye sockets of a skull.

"Quickly now." he said

They were almost to the wrought iron gate with one side fallen and lying on the cavern's grey floor when Boltrein heard a voice call out.

"Hoy! What is such a group as you doing in this part of the city?"

The company held their hoods over their heads and could see a small detachment of armed Illanni dark elf guards approaching them.

Boltrein threw back his hood and snarled. His teeth gleamed white in the darkness.

"That is no concern of yours. Now be off with you," he shouted.

The leader of the guard bowed his head and spoke.

"I am sorry, but I have my orders. What are you doing here, my lord?"

The dark elf vampire took several menacing steps forward, grabbing the guard's chain mail, and hoisted him into the air like a rag doll.

"My business is my own and that is all you need to know," Boltrein said. "Like I commanded, be off with yourself or suffer the consequences."

The other guards clenched their weapons, not sure what Boltrein would do next.

The dark elf guard leader stuttered, "S,s,sorry, my lord. Just doing my duty."

"Well, do it somewhere else," Boltrein snarled.

The troop of guards hurried back the way they had come from and Boltrein waited until they were out of sight before leading the company through the iron gate of the estate. From down the road the leader of the guards peered around the corner of a stone building and caught sight of the last two dwarves entering the gate. The leader of the small patrol then returned to his superior officer to report in.

"It is a mixed lot," he said, "but I am sure I saw two dwarves bring up the rear. It is Lord Boltrein that leads them."

"We'll see what all this is about," the dark elf captain muttered. "Hiding in an abandoned mansion with an odd assortment of companions bodes ill for master Boltrein."

Meanwhile, Boltrein's company had entered the estate and hurried across the polished stone of the entryway. Boltrein motioned to the others and drew his weapon and the others followed suit.

"You never know what might have taken up residence in such an abandoned estate," he said. "Come. Do a quick search while I find another way out."

The company went room by room and found nothing but dusty furniture and the fog that had crept through the lower level windows. Boltrein gathered them all together in one room on the second floor and they removed their hoods. The dangerous trek from the slums had them all sweating heavily despite the chill of the underworld.

Celedant took a step forward.

"Boltrein, if I may."

The Illanni replied, "Go right ahead."

The wizard looked at each of the company, one by one.

"I think we should all be in one room," he told them. "No need to invite disaster by splitting up in such a dangerous place. Our elven and dragon friends can watch over us as we rest. It has been a long night's work and we need food and sleep to end this venture." He turned to Boltrein and asked, "I assume we will reach the temple soon."

"Yes," the dark elf answered, "although how we will reach my father is still a mystery."

The wizard nodded.

"Perhaps one of us will come up with an idea as we rest."

Morganna stood motionless off to the side of the window and watched the street below while the others rested in the room. A few had fallen asleep, and several hushed conversations were going on.

Suddenly she saw a shadow flit across the street, and then more followed and she saw movement on their side of the street as well a band of Illanni dark ones converging on the gate below.

She whispered urgently, "Wake up! The guards are back in force. We need to get out of here."

As the company rose and grabbed their gear, her brother said, "Quickly! Now down the stairs and out the side entrance."

As they all reached the ground floor the front door burst open. Morganna acted out of instinct and summoned her power to cast an invisible wall between the attacking guards and the company. Several dark ones evaded the spell before it was complete and they were on the company's side of the invisible wall attacking the intruders. There were just three of the dark elves, but they proved to be dangerous foes.

Boltrein and Celedant met them and swords clashed as the rest vaulted over the stair's railing. The dark ones slowly succumbed to the swords of Boltrein and Celedant while some of the guards that were behind them ran to attack, but slammed into the spell wall and bounced backwards into their fellow guardsmen.

"Go!" Morganna yelled. It won't hold them long!"

The company followed Boltrein through the house and out the side door towards a gate set in a high wall. As they raced around what used to be a beautiful fountain, the rear gate burst open and the yard was suddenly filled with dark elf guards. Celedant and Inwe lowered their staffs and with his Celedant blew several guards back against the wall and they slumped down unconscious. Inwe's spell was stronger and energy lanced out from her and struck the stone floor of the garden in front of the charging Illanni. Shards of sharp debris were chipped from the stone floor under the plantings and flew into the massed guards. The front rank fell to the courtyard, wounded, and then Boltrein's company threw themselves at the Illanni.

Swords rose and fell. Morganna's blade was a flurry of movement in and out, dancing against the curved sword of one illanni guards. The dark one fell quickly away with a grievous wound and she could see the gate behind it.

At that moment the company heard cries from behind them. Dark elves from the front of the house were coming out the door that led into the garden.

Celedant acted quickly and cast a spell. Ten of the rushing Illanni soldiers froze in mid-stride.

Tarquin and Eldahir had fought through to the gate and now called for the others. Ress and Hority were both fighting a tall dark elf that towered above them. They had been keeping his sword from striking them when Ress stuck him in the chest with her spear. A moment later Hority struck the huge Illanni across the face with his branch and the guard dropped dead.

The guards at the rear of the house were quickly giving way. The company had the upper hand and most of the dark ones had been wounded, but there were still the Illanni coming from the back of the house and weaving through their frozen comrades.

Celedant sent bright orange balls of fire at them to slow them down long enough to shut the gate. Boltrein used his unnatural strength to bend a bar through the locking mechanism and seal the exit.

The remaining Illanni dark elves crashed into the gate, trying to free the lock, but to no avail. One warlock that had been frozen by Celedant made it up to the gate and ordered all the Illanni away. He chanted a spell, touched the lock the metal bar melted before their eyes.

The guards rushed outside but the company had already disappeared into the mist. The guard's captain promised himself that, yes, he would report this fight, but he was going to personally bring lord Boltrein to justice.

•   •   •   •   •

"Come, follow me," Boltrein had called out once he was through the gate. "Our magic will have alerted the vampires and other city guards."

The company dashed off deeper into the city.

After Boltrein was sure they had left the guards far behind, he held up his hand to stop the company.

"I had hoped not to do this, but there is no other course," he said. "We will go to our ancestral home and hide there for the time being."

Morganna's face gave a surprised look that caused him to continue.

"Don't worry. Father has not returned home since mother's death. He resides in the temple now. We will be safe in our home if we are careful."

The company slowed their pace and held their hoods close to their faces. The stone structures around began to grow in size as they advanced deeper into the city. These structures would be considered opulent even above on the surface world. Morganna knew this portion of the city well and recognized when they were close to her old home.

Boltrein slowed to a steady walk and approached an ornate gate guarded by two Illanni in plate mail armor.

He called back over his shoulder to his troops.

"Follow my lead and don't say a word."

Boltrein came to the gate and the two guards responded by saying, "My lord, Boltrein."

He nodded and called cruelly to the others behind him., "Come or your punishment will be severe."

They walked through the empty courtyard and up the front steps. The door was opened by a butler dressed in tight fitting clothes.

"My Lord," he asked, "your company will they be dining with us?"

Boltrein replied disdainfully, "These are an appeasement for my father. They will be locked in the old ballroom. No one is to go near them."

The butler led Boltrein and his company to a huge ballroom with ornate parquet floors and long billowing drapery.

The doors were all locked from the outside. Boltrein paused before closing the last door.

"You will be safe here," he told them. "Once the mists deepen, I will come and get you."

CHAPTER TWENTY-SEVEN

Tibersu was sitting in a large room on the second floor of the temple with a huge balcony overlooking the city and plains below. He was sequestered on the second floor because he deemed himself too important to use the first floor, which was reserved only for his staff and other lackeys.

From his balcony Tibersu heard from some distance away the first horns being blown.

Certainly, this was the army returning from their confrontation with the surface elves. He walked with his dignified posture to the railing and looked far out into the cavern that housed the dark elf capital Illan. There in the distant darkness his eyes could make out the passage the army had taken to confront the elves, and out of it now streamed not a victorious army, but one that appeared routed.

There was no order to the troops. They just flooded out onto the plain hurrying towards the supposed safety of the city.

He spotted the foot soldiers that had to be his cadre of vampires he had sent with general Maglar. They alone showed any sense of calm and they were formed up perfectly, but there were remarkably fewer of them than had ridden out. Had his army, led by his vampires, been so easily beaten, he wondered.

He had to know. The routed army had reached the city and he called for a messenger.

A younger vampire cleric came running and Tibersu demanded, "Go and bring me the leader of our soldiers."

The messenger bowed. "Yes my lord."

Tibersu fumed as he waited and waited and watched the riders returning. Finally, he saw the messenger and an officer of the army walking across the courtyard below him.

Soon the door rang with staccato knocks and he told them to enter and the messenger walked in behind the bloodied soldier. Tibersu could smell the Illanni's fear. With age the messenger would have been able to mask that emotion, but he was still too newly turned.

The other vampire stopped short of Tibersu.

"I bring ill news, my lord," he said,

Tibersu waved the cleric away and the young vampire fairly ran from the room.

"Please," the vampire lord said, "Do tell me what has occurred."

The soldier removed a badly dented helm and Tibersu saw the broken shaft of an arrow protruding from the chain mail near his neck. The vampire's black clothes were torn and covered in blood. Unlike the other routed troops below, Tibersu could see this one had fought bravely against the elves of light. He looked back down and saw that many of them had come to the courtyard and that clerics were walking through the ranks of wounded.

"Our troops fought bravely," the wounded soldier said, "but the surface scum had many wizards and sorceresses in their ranks and their spells were quite effective. The general disappeared early on in the fight and must have fallen to one of the spells cast by the elves. We attacked, but they held. Even when our kind waded into the battle, they were overcome by sheer numbers and were killed. We lost many in the cavern of Docuser. The cavern of death, it should now be called. When the elves began advancing, our ranks failed. First, the cowardly orc scum ran. Despite being cut down by their commanders, they still ran. That started a chain reaction and our warriors fell back. The surface dwellers rained arrows upon us, and their magic users added their cursed fire spells. With our troops out of control, we could no longer face the enemy. We retreated."

Tibersu's anger was evident on his face. He stepped forward suddenly and yanked out the arrow from the soldier's chest. The vampire merely grunted with surprise and Tibersu threw the arrowhead out of the room into the courtyard below.

"I could not stand to look at that elven thing any longer," Tibersu said. "Continue."

The other vampire picked up where it had left off,

"From that moment on we fought throughout our withdrawal. We stood in every cavern or passage wide enough to offer battle, but no matter how many stood our ground, the elves of light brushed us aside. Many of our cowardly soldiers simply surrendered. Our kind stayed on, though, and encouraged our soldiers to fight, but even then the elves pushed us backwards and killed our brethren as they advanced. I have nothing else to report."

Tibersu looked back out from the balcony and saw elves issuing from the far passage where the Illanni had just returned from. He turned to the other vampire.

"I cannot blame those who have been turned. I suppose the battle was lost once the general died. Now, what to do with the elves of light at our front door?"

"We attack them, my lord," the soldier said with a voice full of revenge. "I can get the others and we'll force the unturned Illanni soldiers to attack."

"No," said Tibersu. "They would be as useless as before. I intend you to call all the turned ones you can find. Have them attack the elves on the plain below. There will be no prisoners. Understand?"

The other vampire bowed with a short bob of his body.

"I will gather our forces and drive the scum from our lands."

"Good, go now and may the eyes of Adois be upon you," Tibersu said.

●   ●   ●   ●   ●

After the elves of light exited the tunnel through which they had been chasing the Illanni soldiers, many of the elves were overwhelmed by what they saw before them. Even their generals began suggesting that what lay before them presented a formidable task.

The city rose from a mist and stretched as far as they could see. There were the shrouded lower levels that held thousands of buildings and then, beyond, there were the mansions. The road led onwards through the mist to the middle-sized houses and then to the great houses and estates. Each of them looked like a fortified castle, and these strongholds disappeared back under the darkness of the great cavern's ceiling.

The high elf general Rathar approached Orthorion.

"Do we have enough soldiers to assault this city?" he asked. "I see no wall, but the city itself is larger than we imagined, despite the reports we received from the rebels. We should never have trusted them in the first place."

"I agree," the wood elf general replied. "This task appears too much for even our forces. The rebels would have been used to the city's size and had nothing to compare it to when they gave us their reports. We must remember, though, that Morganna leads a company of renowned adventurers into the heart of the city in an attempt to kill their overlord. If that is accomplished, we may have a chance."

Rathar nodded and said, "If the head of the enemy is severed, I feel that the others will flee. Come. Look yonder, coming out of the mist."

The two generals watched as a small army advanced in the misty distance. These troops were comprised of almost all the vampires that had remained in the city as well as the vampires from the defeated illanni army at Docuser. Suddenly they charged.

General Orthorion called for his ranks to close up and prepare for the assault. The wizards and sorceresses were already casting their spells out at the attackers and the soldiers of Arantir and Trimimar were aligned near the middle of the line to protect both generals. The archers added their weight to the attack, but their arrows did little harm except when striking the approaching enemies in the heart or the head.

It appeared ominous to the generals that their spells and arrows were having little effect upon the racing army.

The rebel Illanni scouts came forth leading several hundred fighters armed with an assortment of weapons. General Orthorion placed these new additions at the right wing of his army and continued to form the other elves for the enemies' final attack.

Only the elves of light's most powerful spells affected the attackers and soon the vampires released spells directed at the defenders' shield wall, making huge gaps in it. The elves of light were tossed aside from the spells and all the while the enemy approached, still at a run.

As the enemy neared the elves, they could distinctly see the fangs of the attackers and suddenly the elves felt the shivers of fear. The oncoming attackers were all vampires. An individual vampire was difficult enough to kill alone, but now a massed army of them approached the elven positions.

The elves' spells had taken some toll as the vampiric tide rushed against them, but it was not enough. The two sides met in a mighty clash and bodies were thrown into the air and then trampled over after they fell back to the cavern floor. Any remnant of order disappeared and the battle turned into a flowing melee. The sides were intermingled, and the vampires blood lust had risen. They slowly overwhelmed the first ranks of the elves, but then the second rank rushed in to attack the vampires while the Illanni rebels circled to take the attackers from the rear.

The elves were slowly losing the battle because it took so many of them to bring down a single vampire, and yet hundreds were attacking. Lucky blows killed some of the vampires, and the elven spells were sometimes effective, but the vampires had so intermingled with the elven army that the spells powerful enough to kill a vampire could not be used for fear of killing their own.

The rear guard, so far proven to be some of the best elven soldiers, were cut right through by the vampiric onslaught. The two captains stood with their soldiers and hacked out at their enemy, but the unnaturally strong vampires surged against their shield wall like a storm tide breaking a sea wall. Many elves of light died in their stalwart defense, but soon they began losing too many soldiers to hold.

Finally, the vampires penetrated far enough into the elves company that their two generals themselves were attacked. They were the best of the best and they fought with style and grace as the vampires rushed them and soon there were several piles of ash lying at their feet as testimony to their skill, but the generals too suffered wounds.

From outside the city a single mournful horn sounded and all the vampires who heard it paused in their attacks.

The halt of the vampires' attack was welcomed by the elves of light and they had a few clicks of the clock to rest before they had to continue fighting.

The vampires listened to the baleful sound of the horn and first one vampire and then another broke from the fight and made their way back towards the city. The elves, mournful of their many dead and wounded, offered no mercy to those fleeing and they attacked the vampires as they retreated through their ranks. Many were killed on their way back through the battlefield.

Once the retreating vampires were clear of the elven forces, their wizards and sorceresses could once again cast their spells. Many running vampires were knocked down and great holes appeared in their ranks. The elven bowmen began to rain down even more arrows into the vampires but to little effect other than to appease them after the deaths of their comrades.

The blood lay thick on the floor of the cavern and the elves were exhausted from their ordeal. Hundreds had been killed and twice as many wounded. There was no way they could advance into the city.

The all-out attack by the vampires had never been foreseen. The rebels had been surprised that such normally solitary creatures would gather in such numbers for the battle, and their generals opined that Tibersu had arranged it.

Slowly the elves of light withdrew to a small rise in the cavern floor and brought their dead and wounded with them. They had for the moment ceased to be an army and they had to reorganize and take care of their wounded. There was no way they could advance into the city with so few hale warriors.

Orthorion knew that his army had been in danger of being overrun by the superior strength and stamina of the vampire horde and he ordered the rear guard to take positions further from the hillock and act as scouts should the vampires return.

Both Trimimar and Arantir, the rearguard commanders, had taken grievous injuries during the attack and they now lay on the ground behind the rise and awaited the healers.

General Orthorion and Rathar hoped that the horn call they had heard had a significance beyond just the recalling of the vampires. Perhaps Morganna had accomplished her mission, they thought, and the vampire's leader was dead.

CHAPTER TWENTY-EIGHT

Boltrein's company was resting quietly in the ballroom when they heard a key turn in the main door's lock. They quickly grabbed their weapons, but it was only Boltrein.

"Come," he said. "The mists are rising and there is bedlam in the streets. The army we saw yesterday was returning from a major defeat. The elves of light won the first battle. Now it is our turn to decapitate the snake."

The company gathered only their weapons and what might be needed in this last battle with Tibersu. Boltrein took them out through a sally port and immediately they ran into soldiers, many looking beaten, and orcs having to be watched over by Illanni troops to keep them from running away. They turned up the street and wound their way through the beaten army, always sure to keep from crossing a vampire.

Boltrein stopped and motioned the band together.

"We are paralleling the main street," he said. "When we reach the temple, we'll have to pass several hundred paces of open area to reach our destination. If you have any plans, that will be where we need to put them in play."

They came to the end of the street and all across the area were unconscious soldiers on the ground or wailing in pain. The Illanni healers were few in number and they had too many to attend to.

"I have a plan with a spell that might be of use," Inwe stated in her formal tone. "It's a transfiguration spell that can make our company look like dark elf Illanni, but I must inform you it is a finicky spell and will fail at the least attempt to speak or move fast. It should work for our purpose of getting to the temple."

In the mists and shadows, she cast her spell and suddenly they all took the shape of an Illanni, at least to anyone's first glance. If they were scrutinized, the aura of the spell could be detected slightly.

Boltrein smiled at the group.

"Come, my dark elves. It is time for the last push," he said.

They began treading their way through the wounded Illanni warriors. There were no vampires to be seen at first, but as they neared the temple, a large group of them exited the building calling to all that were near.

Morganna listened and translated for the others.

"They go to battle the elves of light," she said, "and they are only calling for their brethren, not for the soldiers or their minions."

As if to emphasize her point, the Illanni around them watched the vampires leaving and they slowly got to their feet and hurried away from the courtyard. Many had left their weapons and several healers were carrying their charges off into the mists.

"Their masters leave," Tarquin said, "and the soldiers escape from their duties. It speaks volumes of the state of affairs in Illan. The vampire's rule by terror and the inhabitants do not support them. It is the right time to see what we can do to Tibersu."

The temple doors of the first floor were empty and the promenade, with its huge columns devoid of Illanni dark elves. Morganna grabbed her brother's shoulder.

"Look on the plains below," she told him.

They could see the elven army and the vampires assembling in greater numbers than they could believe.

"It will be a bloody day if we do not succeed," Tarquin said.

Because he spoke too quickly, the spell that Inwe had cast upon him failed and his human form was back. The high elven sorceress looked at him.

"See. I told you it was a fickle spell," she said. "Come. I fear you are right. We must hurry."

The interior of the temple was dark with only a few torches lighting the area.

Boltrein called back, "Come this way through the maze and up the stair to father's new seat of power."

Suddenly guards in plate mail and robed clerics of Adois rushed out of the darkness. Celedant cast a spell that sent electricity at one of the guards, striking his plate mail, and there was a vile burning smell coming from him as he writhed on the floor and slowly turned to ash.

Another guard met the flailing branch of Hority, and it dropped where it stood. The filthy monk dashed away, calling out his familiar war cry "Foes!"

Tarquin faced two vampire clerics as they rushed towards him. He threw Dragon Bolt as the first one attacked and his sword stuck into the vampire's chest. Burning red, it turned the vampire to ash.

Tarquin's weapon continued to burn brightly in the darkened hallway as another vampire closed on him. He stepped slowly forward, dodged the vampire's mace and swung his sword after pulling it free from the ash of the other vampire. He cut twice downwards, his sword hot to the touch, from the vampire's shoulder to hip and set the creature's robe on fire. As it desperately tried to pat out the flames, another vampire cleric came at Tarquin.

He ducked the swing of that cleric's mace and swung again, striking with Dragon Bolt at the legs of his foe. His enemy flopped to the floor and Tarquin chopped downwards and took the head off, ear to ear, with his sword

Several of the other clerics were down, but the one had finished putting out his burning robe. Tarquin could see the charred flesh under the robe, and he attacked it again with vigor. Dragon Bolt was immune to the strength of the vampire's power and Tarquin drove the vampire back until the creature had its back to the wall, desperately trying to fend off Tarquin's blows. Tarquin saw an opening in the vampire's defense and struck once more, severing the head and part of the shoulder from the vampire. It fell in an ashy heap at his feet.

The clerics were dressed only in robes and were easier to kill. Although they were vampires, they carried little in the way of weapons and were quickly surrounded and dispatched. Some fought back, though, and several company members were thrown across the room and landed in heaps against the temple's stone walls.

Other clerics stood back and cast spells at the company. Morganna saw too late one column of flame descending on her, but Azimuth hurriedly cast another spell that deflected the flames from the former dark elf turned wood elf.

Meanwhile, Boltrein, his blood lust rising, was cutting into the priests and slaughtering them left and right.

The company fought with bravery and stood up well to the armored vampires. In most instances, one of their group would concentrate on a frontal assault against a vampire while another, attacking from the rear, was able to decapitate them.

Soon all the vampires that had been guarding the first floor lay in heaps of ash at the company's feet. But at what expense, Morganna wondered. The company had almost all suffered wounds of various types and the healing potions were now quickly passed around. The damage was repaired, but the potions hardly helped the pain of their wounds.

Morganna put her hand on her brother's cold shoulder.

"You need not go further."

Her brother shook his head.

"No. I have set myself down a path that I believe will benefit all of Illan and I will not forgo that. I am a part of this until the end. Come!"

Boltrein led them up the stairs at a slow, silent pace and onto the temple's second floor. A hall bisected the top floor and two giant doors that were closed and led into the main chamber. Five Illanni in full plate mail stood between the company and their goal.

As they reached the top steps, the guards charged. A wicked fight broke out and Hority's battle cry "Foes!" could be heard by all. He was the first to attack a guard and as always his branch topped with a pumice stone struck down the body of the vampire and turned it instantly to ash as its plate mail collapsed on the floor.

Another vampire guard swung its sword and cut deeply into Hority's arm and the monk fell backwards, bumping down the stairs landing in a heap at the bottom of the stairway.

Eldahir and Azimuth took on two of the other guards. Eldahir's sword rang out against one guard's helm while Azimuth picked up the other guards as if he were weightless and bashed its head three times into the wall, pulverizing it. Its ash filled armor dropped onto the ground.

Tarquin had swept the legs out from one of the other Illanni and as his enemy struck the floor, Tarquin severed its neck. The last guard then dove toward Inwe and the two rolled down the steps, entangled together. Elanesse dove after Inwe and ripped the head off the guard. It turned to ash halfway down the stairway.

All that stood in the way of the company now were the golden doors before them.

There was a cry, and all turned to see Inwe, face down at the foot of the stairs, a pool of blood forming under her head and her body in an unnatural position. Hority slid across the polished floor from where he'd fallen, blood pouring from his slashed arm, and he cradled Inwe's head in his lap and began chanting a healing spell. A bright brown light surrounded both elf and dwarf.

Elanesse could tell exactly when her bonded sorceress died. She looked down on the little dwarf trying in vain to heal her and she suddenly felt the bond between herself, as a dragon, and the sorceress slowly sever as Inwe succumbed to her wounds. Elanesse stood on the stairway, bereft, her soul empty. She had been with Inwe for untold years. Then she roared, not as an elf but as a dragon.

Azimuth joined in with Elanesse, sharing in her pain and her roars, and the company had to cover their ears as it grew louder and chunks of the ceiling started to fall from their penetrating howls.

Finally, Elanesse stopped and walked down the stairs to Hority.

"Stand aside, little one," she said in a shaky voice. "She is my burden now."

The company was confused and continued to look down at the grieving dragon.

Hority looking up at the company and shouted.

"Go! We have this under control!"

The others had never heard such a stern voice come from the little dwarf.

•   •   •   •   •

Elanesse slowly bent down, tears flowing from her face and splashing on the bloody floor. She picked up the crushed body of Inwe and began chanting a spell that only Azimuth could understand. He knew it was a spell that could only be used when a dragon or its bond mate died, and he watched as a dark blue mist began forming around their bodies.

When it cleared, they were both gone.

Suddenly Elanesse, the dragon, and her precious Inwe reappeared at the upper most island of the Dragon Isles on the landing ledge of the main dragon eerie. Morphing back into a dragon, she let out a loud keening that was heard throughout the islands and was followed by the echoes of all the dragons present keening with Elanesse.

Even the master wizards at their council meeting deep underground heard it. It was the same sound they had heard only recently from the battles of

Southgard and Dragon Isle. One of their members had died. Telepathically the image of Inwe flashed through the minds of all the masters of the isle.

Soon the masters and their high-ranking wizards called for their dragons and they all began flying north.

As they flew, all the dragons mourned the death of the sorceress Inwe and many of the wizards had tears openly flowing down their faces.

Elanesse had morphed back into her high elf form and was gently laying Inwe's body on a stone slab. Several healing sorceresses that attended the dragons gently spread a bright red silk cloth over the body. The master wizards arrived, and each placed a flower on the red cloth before receding away from the body. Inwe would soon be flown back to her home with a procession of dragons.

It was a time of mourning for all. One of their own had died.

Elanesse morphed back into dragon form and her wings spread out from the body lying on the ground. With one more shriek, her massive head collapsed to the aerie's floor, the loss of her bonded mate too much for her to bear. The link they had shared for so many eons was gone and neither Elanesse's mind or her body could regain control.

Several dragons rushed to her side. They knew what dire trouble she was in and they had seen dragons who lost their bonded ones throwing themselves off a cliff to the jagged rocks below or opening a rift into the void and disappearing forever. Sometimes they became so deranged that they had to be kept like prisoners in the deepest caves of the aerie.

Two dragons surrounded Elanesse and cooed to her themselves to show they understood the loss of ties only bonded ones could feel. They placed their wings over Elanesse's body and rubbed their heads along her neck as they began leading her further inside the aerie and away from Inwe's body.

Their constant cooing helped ease some of the sorrow Elanesse felt and let her know that the whole aerie was there to aid her in her time of need. She was led deep into the caverns, always in contact with other dragons, until she collapsed onto her side. The old blue healing dragon came up to her then and murmured spells while her two sorceresses' helpers reached to get the right powders and magical healing potions from the blue dragon's side pouches.

• • • • •

Hority quickly wrapped a bandage on his bleeding arm. It had partly healed when he had tried to save Inwe. Afterwards he had followed the others crawling up the steps one at a time, but he had heard nothing of the dragon's roar. Hority was in too deep a trance trying to heal the dying elf. He had just assumed there was a battle taking place and that he had to be in it for Clor's sake.

Following Elanesse's cry of sorrow, Boltrein led the company up to the door and shoved against it with all his vampiric might. The doors opened easily, and the company was greeted by the sight of Tibersu and ten more of his personal guards, all vampires.

Tibersu smiled at them, his sharp fangs easily seen in the flickering torch light.

"Ah, my daughter and son-in-law are here to attend the death of an army," he said. "My crowning achievement as of yet. Ah, my son. Once I had tasted your blood, I always knew you were weak. A betrayal, after I gave you immortality. That is just shameful. I also just heard one of your dragon ilk as it perished."

Morganna began to speak and her friends spread out around her, their weapons drawn.

"Father call off this obsession. Taza is dead. Throw off his yoke. Our people need you with your full senses...they don't need a blood thirsty and uncaring tyrant."

"You are so young," he replied. "So ignorant of the world about you. I offer our people freedom and a new way of life. Soon the surface elves will feel the full, pure power that we can yield not just the puny attacks I have sent out."

Celedant said, "There is still a chance for you all to live together in peace."

Tibersu snarled an animalistic grunt.

"I did not give you permission to speak, human," Tibersu told him and with a flick of his hand he sent Celedant hurdling across the marble floor to the wall. His head struck against it and he fell dazed to the floor.

Tibersu's ring burned mightily with the effort, another power that the ring had now decided to unveil.

"Come," Tibersu said. "I have a battle to watch and I grow weary of this conversation."

Before anyone could speak, from his kneeling position Celedant sent forth a rush of flames from his staff which engulfed two of the vampire guards. The rest rushed the company while Tibersu looked on with a smile on his evil face and his elongated teeth showing prominently.

The remaining vampires crashed into the company. Tarquin faced one that attacked him silently, but as Tarquin swung at its head, it slipped under his blade and struck Tarquin in his side. He grasped the vampire's pommel with all his strength and held the blade steady before countering the attack and cutting back handed to sever the vampire's head. The now blazing Dragon Bolt cut completely through the plate mail helmet.

Tarquin then fell backwards and lay on the floor in excruciating pain while trying to pull the vampire's sword from his side.

Boltrein was locked in hand to hand struggle with one of the guards while Morganna and Eldahir fought against their two attackers. It did not appear that they would win the fight until Ress's spear struck into one vampire guard's underarm. She pulled it out, bloodied from the vampire fighting Eldahir. The elf could then quickly and cleanly pivot and he swung his blade and took the vampire's arm off at the shoulder. With a neat pirouetting reversal, Eldahir than decapitated the creature.

One vampire had its hand around Morganna's throat and her feet flailed out against the floor underneath her as the vampire slowly squeezed the life from her. Azimuth ran to the suffocating wood elf, slammed into the vampire from the rear and slowly pulling him down to allowing Morganna to escape from its clutches. With his draconic strength Azimuth then ripped the head off of the vampire and ended its cold existence.

Celedant stood and lowered his staff to summon the power of the stone around him. Bright balls of flame shot out and violently slapped two of the vampires in the chest, burning a hole all the way through their armor and their torsos and out the back plate.

The two vampires were then quickly overcome by other members of the company who momentarily had stared at the wizard in wonder. His actions forever surprised them.

Tarquin lay against the wall, still pulling on the sword in his side as a dark shadow loomed up before him. One of the last remaining vampires was going in for the easy kill. Tarquin took up his own sword and swung it out at the vampire, but the powerful vampire made Dragon Bolt dance back out of the way.

Suddenly Ress appeared, a bloodied spear clasped in both her hands. She confronted the vampire and the Illanni thrust its sword, but Ress easily blocked it with the spear's shaft. She followed with a strong thrust of her own against its armor encased body and the vampire nearly lost its balance.

Tarquin had eased himself to a standing position, his back to the wall, while Ress battled the monster. Suddenly from over her shoulder Tarquin's dagger flew by her and struck the vampire in the eye. The thin blade entered its brain and dropped it to the floor, completely in shock. To make sure of the kill Ress thrust her spear through the thing's neck as the creature slumped down and pinned it to the floor. With his sword Tarquin then struck off its head before he himself fell back down, blood oozing from around the blade still in his side.

Boltrein and his attacker rolled around on the floor, each fighting to gain an advantage. They used their fangs as well as their hands and legs as weapons. Boltrein had kept blocking all the attacks, but the Illanni gained control by sitting atop Boltrein. It drew its dagger. Boltrein grabbed the plunging dagger and diverted it from his face enough that it slammed hard into his shoulder. Without a grunt of pain Morganna's brother grasped the dagger and using all his strength turned the blade back into the face of the vampire. Boltrein moved his legs into a good position and was able to flip his attacker over and off him. One more quick movement of his body and Boltrein landed on top of his vampire opponent. The attacker lay still and Boltrein saw the dagger had lodged hilt deep into its heart.

Meanwhile Eldahir reached for his own dagger and sliced through the throat and spinal cord of his adversary. The last vampire seeing how its fellows had died ran and jumped off the balcony to land in the plaza below and lope off into the darkness.

Morganna stood and faced her father.

"Stop this insanity!" she yelled at him.

Eldahir sent an arrow flying toward Tibersu, but with a simple wave of his hand the arrow was deflected. The ring burned his finger incredibly and had once again shown off its latent abilities, once again with painful consequences to Tibersu.

Tibersu laughed and grasped his necklace and was suddenly enshrouded in a red glow.

Already my army is decimating the elves," he said. "Soon my forces will begin adventuring above ground."

"No, I cannot allow that father," Morganna said.

The amulet gifted by the black dragon now flared bright red. Tibersu spoke a word of power and pushed with his hand. His daughter flew backwards and crashed against the toppled statue of Taza.

Tibersu was about to cast another rush of energy with his amulet when Celedant sent a lightning bolt shooting towards him. The amulet's red dome sent the lightning bolt shooting back at the caster and it struck in front of Celedant and thrust the wizard backwards, his clothes afire.

Tibersu began another incantation, but Azimuth recognized the spell and reacted immediately to form an invisible barrier in front of his company. The spell that Tibersu had cast sent a vast cloud of ice streaming towards them, but it was blocked by the counter spell.

Azimuth dove around the side of the barrier and lined up to cast another spell at Tibersu. The dark elf was concentrating on his own spell and never saw the dragon's spell. Ten orcs magically appeared around Tibersu and attacked him from all directions. The vampire lord held up his ring to add power to the red shield, and the orc's weapons could not penetrate the new red barrier, but just bounced off of it. With a single movement Tibersu sent out a red shimmer of small bolts at the orcs and they died instantly, disappearing in tiny puffs of smoke.

Eldahir ran at the vampire and was followed closely by Boltrein. Swinging their swords, they clanged into Tibersu's red globe in a clashing loud enough to be heard in the plaza below. Eldahir and Boltrein fought bravely, but against such a powerful magical energy, there was little they could do. They were soon on the defensive. Tibersu's sword emerged from the red spell and broke through Eldahir's defense and sliced through the armor across the elf's chest. Eldahir was thrown backwards and lay still on the stone floor.

Boltrein took to the offensive and struck again and again at his father, but always his sword just clanged against the red mist. Celedant, kneeling where he had been thrown, saw that an amulet around Tibersu's neck was also now burning bright red. He waited. Tibersu struck out at his son and snapped Boltrein's blade in half and he crashed to the floor.

Celedant knew he had to get his spell exactly right and send it towards Tibersu at just the right moment. His bright blue beam struck the tip of the dark one's sword and flowed through its red encasement as it struck Tibersu in the chest. The dark elf looked down at his amulet as it exploded, throwing the vampire backwards.

Boltrein was now bruised and exhausted. Then Tibersu picked up his son and threw him to the ground. He raised his sword above his head for the coup-de-gras. Tibersu looked over and saw Celedant approaching with his staff lowered. The Illanni's eyes widened and the wizard cast another spell. Electricity arced through the air to Tibersu and the shock surged through him. He stood straight up with the electricity running up and down his body. Only the balustrade kept him from falling to the court below and only his magical ring kept him from being burned alive.

A bolt of fire then struck Tibersu in his upper right torso and blasted his arm into oblivion, leaving a deep wound that showed his charred ribs. It also blew off the finger that had been holding his ring.

In the doorway stood a wavering Hority. The dwarf then crashed to the ground from blood loss after casting his mighty spell.

Celedant followed up next by sending a deluge of small red balls at the vampire. They exploded on contact and shredded the monster's armor and blistered the skin below.

Azimuth then used his dragon magic to attack with a bright, narrow flame shooting out from his finger. It struck Tibersu directly in the face and his skin hung in charred patches, the bone beneath showing. The Illanni grasped the balustrade for support with his one remaining arm.

Seeing her father savaged, Morganna cried out. Even if she hated him, she still hung onto the hope that he would come around to her side.

Celedant followed with one more spell this, a precise energy bolt that shot straight from his staff to Tibersu's chest. The energy spear burst through his torso, piercing the Illanni's chest and tossing the vampire backwards over the railing. He landed face down in the courtyard below.

Morganna jumped down after her father as she cast the very spell she had used to escape being turned. She floated down to the courtyard below, landed and stood next to her father. Tibersu looked into her eyes. All she saw was vile evil.

The skin hanging from Tibersu's face had already begun to heal when she raised her bloodied sword to sweep off her father's head. As she did, the Illanni leader thrust his sword through his daughter's stomach. She took several steps backwards before collapsing to the courtyard. Her blood pooled around her body.

All the others were staring out at the battle and paying Tibersu little or no attention. Morganna was down and hopefully dead. He struggled to withstand his pain, which was incredible even for a vampire, and he decided to take his chance to escape.

Suddenly Botreg stood there in front of him, grinning in the darkness.

"Thought ye were going to reach safety?" he asked.

Tibersu shot out his left hand so fast that Botreg never saw it coming and Tibersu grasped the dwarf and hurled him out into the fog. Just as Botreg was being thrown, he brought out his dagger and slammed it into the dark elf's thigh. Tibersu launched the pest of a dwarf away into the dark fog and never noticed the dagger, poison spread all across its blade.

When Tibersu finally began to run into the darkness, he felt the weapon and quickly withdrew it and tossed it into the fog. As he stumbled out into the darkness, he could feel the wounded parts of his body healing itself, but he began feeling odd and soon he was stumbling, first to his right and then his left.

He did not notice that he had been poisoned, but his vampire self-healing took over and the stab wound suddenly oozed out the poison. The dark lord began to feel better.

Soon he got his legs under him again and he began a full out run. He quickly found a small tunnel going up into the cavern rock and he ducked into it.

He started climbing up with the one arm he had left.

CHAPTER TWENTY-NINE

Boltrein picked himself up and retrieved a gem encrusted horn he found hanging from the balustrade on a gold chain. The horn of Adois had been used to summon all the turned ones to the temple for special occasions and standing at the railing, Boltrein began blowing the horn in an intricate signal. He repeated the call until his exhausted body could no longer exhale. Even a vampire had its limits and fighting his father had drained him of his strength.

Eldahir was still bleeding from his chest as he stood at the rail holding on to one column.

"The vampires retreat. They are retreating," he called out,

"I sounded the call that Tibersu was dead," Boltrein said and smiled. "They have given up. They might be revenge minded, though, so I think we should get out of here and go back to my father's estate."

Only then did he see his sister lying in a pool of blood in the courtyard. There was no sign of his father.

Azimuth came up to Boltrein holding Celedant upright. He had slammed into the stone wall and was still patting out the small fires consuming his clothes. Eldahir was wounded from a sword blow that had penetrated his defenses and sliced through his armor deep into his chest. Hority was barely conscious but was helping Tarquin stand despite the deep wound in his own arm.

Seeing Morganna, Boltrein jumped from the second story of the temple and landed effortlessly next to his sister. Her face, pale from the blood lost, grimaced from the pain she was in. He took out a vial and poured a little in the entrance wound and a little on her back before cradling her and helping her up.

"That will ease the pain and begin to heal it," he said softly to her, "but we need a healer quickly."

Suddenly Eldahir was by his side, having run as fast as a wounded elf could from the balcony to be with his wife. He gently pulled her to him and placed her head on his shoulder.

Boltrein called up to the others.

"Get down here! We need healers quickly before all the vampires in Illan show up."

Once they were all assembled in the courtyard, Boltrein looked over the company. They were in disarray and tired from their dash through the slums with no rest and now they nearly all were seriously wounded from a fight with Tibersu and his vampire minions.

Botreg stepped forward out of the fog.

"Tibersu has escaped even though I poisoned him. There is no telling if it will work on a vampire."

Boltrein grasping his sister's hand and said, "Come. We must hurry. I can get healers aplenty once we are in the estate."

The company made a quick retreat from the temple to the courtyard of Tibersu's estate.

All around them was panic. The Illanni soldiers were in a state of turmoil while the orcs were all making a run for it through the city and to the passages beyond deep in the cavern behind the estates.

● ● ● ● ●

Boltrein led the company to his father's house and the panicky guards stopped him at the gate.

"My lord, what should we do?" The lead guard asked. "We heard the recall of the army. There is rioting in the streets."

The new lord of the estate looked around. The household staff had all gathered, not even questioning the appearance of his strange friends.

"Bar the gates till I can sort things out," Boltrein told them. "Only let in those you know…and no allies of my father. Call me to speak to them. Everything will subside and we will soon be all right."

He turned to a tall Illanni dressed in immaculate black clothes.

"Could you be so kind as to fetch several healers?" he asked him.

"Ah, I'm a healer," Hority piped up behind Boltrein in a hurtful voice.

The Illanni head of the household bowed to the dusty and bloodied dwarf.

"But of course, sir. I had forgotten in the recent excitement. I did not know if you were exhausted after healing your arm and taking care of Inwe. Both must have been such deep cuts to both your ability and your psyche."

Hority sighed, "Ye are probably right. This has tired me. The death of Inwe was difficult on me. I might need help."

Tarquin was still being held up by Hority and Botreg.

"There was nothing you could do for Inwe," he told Hority. "She was too far gone to be called back to this world. She is now with the gods."

Hority was sobbing at his inability to save the high elf. Tarquin placed a hand on the monk's dirty habit.

Boltrein dismissed the household staff to return to their duties and led the rest of his company into the house.

"We will go to the topmost floor and watch what is happening," he said. "The vampires should be here about now looking for their fallen leader."

CHAPTER THIRTY

The company had climbed the several stories to the upper most rooms of the house and from that vantage point they could look out over the cavern and into the streets below. The bloodied remains of the vampire army had already reached the courtyard of the temple and found their lord missing.

Out on the plains of the cavern Boltrein could make out the elven army retreating with their wounded and dead to the mouth of the large passage that led into the cavern. Those that could still fight had been assembled on the small rise.

"They have suffered such casualties fighting the vampires that they have had to retreat," Celedant said sadly.

The Castilian dressed in his formal black attire soon came to Boltrein with another Illanni, his clothes rumpled and blood-stained.

Boltrein simply said, "See to my friends."

The healer stood there in shock and stuttered, "They are outsiders."

Boltrein turned and bared his teeth, "See to them quickly now…unless I have to pitch you out the window and call another of your ilk."

The healer went to work immediately and soon Tarquin and Morganna had their wounds bound tightly and were feeling well enough to join Boltrein at the window. The wounds of Eldahir and Hority were covered with a healing poultice and bandaged up. The two lay comfortably on the plush rug.

"I have done what I can," the cleric said. "I have been tasked sorely this night."

"I will see to these wounded, as well," Azimuth added,

"What now, brother?" Morganna asked.

He smiled at her.

"I have not the foggiest idea."

They heard a hurried knock on the door and a harried guard entered and stood at attention before them.

"My lord," he said, "there is a delegation of nobles at the gate asking to speak to the new master."

Morganna and her brother gave each other curious glances.

"I wonder what this is all about," Boltrein said.

•   •   •   •   •

Boltrein strode slowly but purposefully towards the gate like as if he had not a worry in the world. He noticed through the iron gates that the delegation looked harried and some had frightened looks on their faces. Not all in the group were vampires, but many were.

Stopping at the gate he asked, "What seems to be the problem?"

There were several answers all at once and then a short, stout Illanni vampire calmed the crowd and spoke.

"Lord Tibersu is missing. The elves camp on our doorstep. What are we to do?"

"Why do you come to me with such questions?" Boltrein asked.

The short Illanni vampire said, "Your father has abandoned us. We look to you for answers."

"Humm," Boltrein mused. "You are giving me command of the city?"

Another illanni said, "The leadership follows the male line. Now you are our clan leader."

"I will go and speak to the elves," Boltrein said. "Our city may yet be saved and the bloodshed stopped. What do you say to that?"

The unturned Illanni dark ones and the vampires all looked stunned.

"You would speak to the elves?" the short one asked. "They would surely kill you before they would enter into discussions."

"I have hope that they will act otherwise." Boltrein responded. "Their actions are for the attacks orchestrated by my father, not by me. Now that my father is gone, I feel that we may be able to work out a lasting peace."

The gathered crowd seemed to remain unnerved about Boltrein's solution.

"Those of you that support me may ride out to the elves," Boltrein told them. "Those that don't had better leave the city at once because once peace is resolved, there will be no place safe enough for my rivals." He turned and called out, "Horses for me and my companions. Any who support me and want to represent the city are welcome to come. I leave as soon as possible."

His guards saddled enough horses in the stable for Boltrein's friends and for ten guards to accompany him. By the time they were ready, the street was crowded with Illanni on horseback and afoot.

Morganna grasped her reins and leaned over to her brother and whispered, "A white flag may be needed."

"An odd practice, certainly," Boltrein said, "We were never a race for peace and certainly were never in a position of defeat."

Eldahir and Hority both had mounted, still in pain from their wounds, but they would not miss what was going to happen.

"T'will be an astonishing act as there ever was," Hority said to Eldahir.

Boltrein rode out of the gates with Morganna at his side, followed by his entourage. They had only gone several blocks when they heard a voice shout out, "Traitor!" and a body rushed out of the dark at Boltrein. He quickly drew his sword, parried the attacker's blow and neatly brought down his blade on the dark elf's head. The vampire reeled away and several of the lord's new followers finished the creature off.

The company continued riding and walking slowly down the main thoroughfare out onto the plain before the city. Boltrein could see how many elves of light remained upon the battlefield. If not for his call on the horn, he was sure all the elves would have been slain to the last soldier.

As they approached the battle-weary elves, a single arrow arched out and landed fifty paces in front of them and slid across the stone to halt at their feet.

Boltrein waved a white flag and heard a lot of stirring in the elven camp. They had all taken up weapons and stood ready for a fight, but the white flag intrigued them. Soon fifty elves, weapons drawn, and arrows notched, walked through their lines and towards the Illanni delegation.

Boltrein and his company dismounted and walked to greet them. With hidden smiles General Orthorion and General Rathar watched them approach. They knew that Morganna's mission had been accomplished and that it had been these brave souls who had sounded the retreat.

Morganna stepped forward and shook hands with the generals.

"May I introduce you to Lord Boltrein, the new leader of the Illanni clans," she said.

Boltrein bowed and added, "At least to the majority of the Illanni. It is a pleasure to meet in peace with our brethren from the surface world."

Orthorion bowed as well.

"It is a pleasure not to be fighting any longer…even if it is a dubious pleasure to be negotiating with a vampire."

"General," Morganna assured him, "Boltrein—like many of our people—was turned against his will and was forced to follow the ways of Taza and then of my father."

"No one need fear me," Boltrein said. "I have never fed on Illanni blood or any others'. I have only appeased my hunger with animal blood."

"Well, then," General Rathar bluntly asked, "Why are you here?"

The new lord bowed to the general.

"I am here to surrender our city. Our people are in turmoil and lost after my father's disappearance. His army has fallen apart. The vampires that attacked you have either fled or are in the city, but they are no longer controlled by my father's power."

"Generals, the city is in a state of flux," Morganna added. "You may find danger there, but it has surrendered. Act as you want. My brother will cooperate."

"I never thought to trust an Illanni," Rathar said to general Orthorion, "but Morganna has proved me wrong. I must admit our army has yet to recover from the last attack. There is no way for us to take control of the city."

"You don't need to," Boltrein said. "Half the city wishes to return to the surface while the other half is still dubious about the land above. My sister and the rebels have proven that point."

He looked squarely at the two generals to be sure they would grasp what he was about to say.

"I will consolidate my power in the city and offer an escort to the rebels the ones that wish to leave immediately. Others will follow once word reaches us about life above ground. Of that I am sure. The vampires I cannot vouch for. I will control those in the city, but many have already taken flight and more will do so in the coming weeks."

The generals conferred for a click of the clock and then Orthorion spoke.

"We agree with the terms but ask that you limit the number of vampires that try to escape. I would hate to think of the trouble they may cause in the future."

Boltrein bowed again to the two generals.

"I will endeavor to follow your demands. I would invite you to enter the city, but I cannot vouch for your safety for I myself was attacked as I rode through the streets. But rest assured, the army will be on my side and order will be restored with as little damage as possible. You will have no fear from this city again."

CHAPTER THIRTY-ONE

Morganna hugged her brother and bade him a tearful goodbye.

The company followed Morganna as she walked towards the elven army. Ress was helping Tarquin walk, her arm grasping his arm, her head on his shoulder. Morganna was doing the same for Eldahir.

The generals stayed and talked about more details of the peace treaty as Morganna and her company moved toward the elven lines.

There were smiles on the otherwise stoic faces of the elves. They knew that they still lived in no little thanks to these heroes. Tarquin's company looked the worse for wear, their clothes covered in blood and with other signs that they had all been in a colossal fight.

The first lines of the elven army parted and the company saw what little remained of them. Barely four hundred elves guarded the opening at the edge of the cavern, and most of them lay recuperating after their healing spells in the passage. The company found the remainder of the rebels guarding the other end of the passage and in another cavern filled with wounded.

Morganna received a rousing cheer as they walked forward through the dark elves. The long-awaited day had come. The Illanni people were free.

•　　　•　　　•　　　•　　　•

Tibersu had climbed and climbed up the narrow passage. He did not care where it terminated as long as he was out of Illan. He had been beaten overthrown by that vile elf loving son of his.

The tunnel suddenly opened up into a cavern and he waited a considerate time before venturing forth. The healing of his chest was nearly complete, but somehow he knew that he had lost his arm forever. The spell that blew it off had been fire based, and his chest was healing too slowly. He still felt dizzy and he wondered if all the poison had been expelled.

He stumbled along against the boulders in the passage until he could see the light of day at the end of the tunnel.

Finally, he felt safe and he sat down, his back to a boulder.

His plan had failed, he knew. What he didn't know yet was what his next move would be.

CHAPTER THIRTY-ONE

The company of white orcs watched intently as the remainder of the army exited the cave with their hundreds of wounded elves and barely half of the soldiers that had first entered the underworld. The leader of the orcs knew that his company numbered only a hundred and would have no chance in winning a fight with this army, however few of them were left. He rolled over and contacted Cyra, the black witch, using the magical device.

Her voice issued forth from the magical item.

"What has occurred?" she asked him. "Are the dreaded ones dead?"

The commander told her, "They have issued forth from the cave, but they are accompanied by too many elves for us to attack. We would never even get close to them before we would be cut down by elven arrows. They are, however, missing, three of their company."

Cyra, many miles away, nodded her head.

"A wise decision," she said. "They will investigate the earlier attack. We will have them then. You may return."

ABOUT THE AUTHOR

Steve Stephenson has published an epic fantasy trilogy. He gravitates for inspiration toward writers such as JRR Tolkien, Raymond Fiest, and Terry Brooks. Steve graduated with a BA in history and a master's in library science. He is an avid book collector of fantasy and science fiction. Also, he sells antiquarian book estates.

NOTE FROM THE AUTHOR

Word-of-mouth is crucial for any author to succeed. If you enjoyed *Vampire Brother*, please leave a review online—anywhere you are able. Even if it's just a sentence or two. It would make all the difference and would be very much appreciated.

Thanks!
Steve Stephenson

We hope you enjoyed reading this title from:

BLACK ROSE
writing™

www.blackrosewriting.com

Subscribe to our mailing list – *The Rosevine* – and receive
FREE books, daily deals, and stay current with news about
upcoming releases and our hottest authors.
Scan the QR code below to sign up.

Already a subscriber? Please accept a sincere thank you for
being a fan of Black Rose Writing authors.

View other Black Rose Writing titles at
www.blackrosewriting.com/books and use promo code
PRINT to receive a **20% discount** when purchasing.